CAPTAIN McRAE

The Missouri River is the gateway to the West: a thousand miles of mud, sudden torrents, treacherous currents, hidden snags, unexpected inlets, hostile Indians hidden behind every bend. And Captain Brant McRae knows every turn in it like the back of his hand. When his boat burns at its dock, strangers hire him to pilot the Western Star up the Big Muddy. McRae suspects there's something sinister about this job — but not that he carries a contraband cargo . . .

WILLIAM HEUMAN

CAPTAIN MCRAE

Complete and Unabridged

LINFORD
Leicester

First published in the United States by
William Morrow & Co.

First Linford Edition
published 2021
by arrangement with
Golden West Literary Agency

There is sound historical basis for the general action
of this narrative, although none of the incidents as
related actually happened, and all the characters
are fictitious.

A catalogue record for this book is available
from the British Library.

ISBN 978–1–78541–964–5

Published by
Ulverscroft Limited
Anstey, Leicestershire

Printed and bound in Great Britain by
TJ Books Ltd., Padstow, Cornwall

This book is printed on acid-free paper

To my brother Bob

1

At four o'clock in the afternoon, Brant McRae turned his back on the river and walked woodenly back to town. Eight years of dreaming, sweating and saving were going up in smoke behind him.

Fifteen hundred people lining the east bank of the upper Missouri, and crowding the wharfs of Dakota City, watched him go in silence. They looked at him, and they looked at his boat, and no one spoke as he passed, face and hands blackened, eyebrows singed from the two hours he'd battled the blaze, fighting the red fury which had licked up the sides of his beautiful white Missouri packet, the *Cairo Lady*.

He heard a man say softly behind him, 'There she goes.' He didn't turn to look. Tall, heavy-shouldered frame erect, hands swinging at his sides, Brant turned left when he reached the main street, a deserted street with every man, woman and child down at the water's edge watching the boat burn.

He did hear the roar and sizzle as the *Cairo Lady* took her last plunge, settling in thirty feet of water at the wharf where she'd been tied. Part of her superstructure would remain above water, and her flags would wave from the jack staff, but it would only be a mockery.

Brant McRae flinched when he heard that roaring sound behind him. He closed his eyes, clenched his fists, relaxed them, and then stepped into the Dakota Queen Saloon. It was empty save for one bartender, the fat-faced, blunt-nosed Jake Brewer, who was slapping at the bar with a rag. The Dakota Queen normally had four bartenders behind the mahogany, but three of them were down at the water's edge.

Brewer looked up, nodding briefly as Brant put both elbows on the wood, clasping his hands together.

'Whiskey,' Brant said.

Jake Brewer put a bottle and a glass in front of him without a word, his fat face expressionless.

Brant poured the first drink, downed it, and then poured another and downed that. When he was filling the glass the third time, the bartender's eyebrows lifted slightly. In this tough river town Jake Brewer was accustomed to occasional fast-drinking customers, but he'd never seen anything like this. He said thoughtfully, 'Tough, Mr. McRae.'

Brant just looked at him as he set the bottle down, and Brewer wisely ambled away. After the fourth drink, the bottle which had been partially filled, was empty. Brant slapped his big fist on the bar and Brewer came back, looked at him, and got another full bottle from the shelf. He set it down in front of the lone drinker and moved away again.

The crowd started to drift in as Brant worked on this second bottle. Several men came toward him, but Brewer, standing halfway down toward the other end of the bar, waved them away frantically.

In a few minutes the long mahogany bar was jammed, but Brant McRae drank alone, space for at least two drinkers on either side of him. He didn't seem to notice the anomaly. After a while Brewer passed him and he said, 'How much?'

'Dollar an' a quarter.' Brewer figured. 'I'm taking the bottle,' Brant said.

'Two dollars,' Brewer said and he put the cork into the bottle, picking up the bills Brant shoved toward him. 'Take it easy, Mr. McRae,' he said.

The bottle under his arm, Brant turned and walked toward the door, his steps steady, a miracle in itself. He saw heads turn furtively to watch him, but no one spoke, knowing what he was doing, knowing that they would do the same if they'd been in his position.

The crowd on the porch opened up as he came through the bat-wing doors, but the passage between them was quite narrow. Another man was coming through the crowd, and as Brant walked steadily forward like a man wading through waist-high water, he hit this man with his right shoulder, spinning him around. He kept walking, not even turning his head to look. He walked east in the direction of the hotel, the whiskey bottle tucked under his arm, a big man with a smoke-blackened face, the whites of his eyes showing distinctly, his mouth a thin, straight line.

He'd lost his hat in the fight against the fire, and his black hair was ruffled. He smelled of smoke, and smoke from his burning packet boat was still in the air. It hung there above Dakota City making the atmosphere even more hot and humid, a grim reminder to Brant McRae that a dream is a dream, and that a man must awaken from all of them.

He'd had a dream years ago, when he was a tough young roustabout on the New Orleans levee. He would pilot his own packet boat some day. He would stand with the hickory spokes of the wheel in his hands, and watch the big river roll down at him.

Eight years had gone into the dream, and he'd planned it carefully and coolly.

The big money on the Mississippi lay in piloting, and he'd taken the abuse of surly, arrogant licensed pilots for three years, serving as cub pilot, learning the river before finally receiving his own license from the commission. He'd spent two years on the Mississippi, and then three more on the turbulent Big Muddy, the upper Missouri, where pilots were making the real money, He'd learned every mile of it from New Orleans to Fort Adams, three thousand miles of muddy water. He could run it in broad daylight, and he could run it at night with only a star, a ridge, a shadow or a dead tree to guide him.

For eight years he'd bucked the river up in that lonely pilot house. He'd taken a Sioux arrow in his shoulder at Disaster Bend, favorite ambush of the upper river Indians; twice he'd been blown up with his boats when ambitious captains had tied down the safety valves and piled on the steam in attempts to shatter records for particular runs.

He'd come through it, and he'd purchased his boat, the three boiler *Cairo Lady*, fastest packet on the upper Missouri. He'd handled her as a pilot, and he knew what she could do. Two years before he'd decided upon the *Cairo Lady*, and then suddenly she was his, and then thirty days later the river had claimed her, and he was back where he'd been eight years before.

No one had been to blame as far as he knew. There had been no carelessness on his part, nor the part of the crew, but still the fire had broken out, and in a boat as well-ordered as his own, it was mystifying. All during the hours that he'd fought the flames this had been on his mind.

The *Cairo Lady* had come up from St. Louis two days before, and lay tied at the wharf in Dakota City. His engineer had kept up steam in the boilers because they'd planned on leaving for Fort Adams and the upper river immediately. Fire did not usually break out on a boat with its fires banked. If they'd been out in mid-river bucking the strong current, with the steam whistling through the gauges, it would have been different, but with banked fires —

His solid jaws set tight, and bitterness in his gray eyes, Brant walked down the street toward the hotel. The liquor he'd already drunk burned his insides, but it did not take away the sting. His mind, strangely enough, was still clear, and it was the mind he'd been trying to deaden in the Dakota Queen Saloon.

A small knot of men stood on the corner, a block from the hotel, discussing the fire. They stared at him as he came up, opening to let him go through. He didn't speak, and none of them spoke to him, nor did he see the furtive, sly expressions that passed between two of them standing on the outer edge of the crowd before they quickly turned and walked away in the opposite direction.

The others, who knew him and respected him, looked at his face, and they left him alone, understanding the mood he was in.

At the next corner, crossing the street to the Grant Hotel, he saw the girl on the porch. She'd evidently just come through the doorway to the edge of the steps and was standing there when she saw him coming toward her, the liquor bottle in the hollow of his right arm, hatless, his face and arms smudged from the fire.

Brant slowed down, and he looked up at her from the bottom step of the hotel porch as she stood there in her white dress, with a tiny straw bonnet on her head. There were touches of blue in the dress, and a blue ribbon in the bonnet to bring out the color of her eyes, a light, powdery blue. Her hair was light brown, almost honey-colored, done up in ringlets, and she carried a tiny blue parasol.

She looked down at him, and he expected her to be shocked because she was evidently an eastern girl just landed at this river town, and be was not a pretty sight to meet even in broad daylight. The girl with the straw bonnet was not shocked. A slight, sympathetic smile played around the corners of her mouth.

She knew who he was, and she knew why he was drinking.

They'd been fighting the fire on the *Cairo Lady* long enough for the story to have circulated through town. This girl may have seen him in the hotel that morning before the fire broke out. At any rate she knew who he was, and she did not censure him. It was a nice thing.

Brant stood there, swaying very slightly, and then he made a slight bow, realizing how ridiculous he looked and how ridiculous it was to be formal at a time like this. He said slowly, steadily, no slur to his speech even now, 'Madam, I regret having to meet you under such circumstances.'

He watched her twirl the parasol around once before she spoke, and when she spoke her voice was low, musical, not the twang of New England, nor the broad A of the middle border states. He placed her from the northern states of the Confederacy. Possibly, Virginia, or even Maryland. She said softly, 'I understand, Captain.'

'I should like,' Brant McRae went on, taking a firmer grip on the bottle, 'to apologize for my appearance at this time. It is not my custom to walk the streets of Dakota City with a liquor bottle under my arm, nor this much liquor inside of me.'

A hint of amusement came to her blue eyes. She said, 'I am sure of that, Captain, and now may I make a suggestion?' Brant bowed solemnly. He spread his legs a little to steady himself because the liquor and the hot sun overhead were beginning to unsettle him. 'I am at your service, madam,' he said.

'Throw away that bottle,' the girl advised. 'Sleep for twenty-four hours and then see what kind of a man you are when you wake up.'

Brant grinned as he started up the steps. 'The sleep will come,' he chuckled, 'when the bottle is empty.' He held up the bottle as he went past her and he said, 'This is all I have left, madam.'

'No,' the girl in the white dress told him quietly. 'You've only lost your boat, Captain. *You* are still left.'

Brant paused as he stood beside her, looking down into her face curiously. She did not shrink away from him, but returned his gaze steadily.

'You are a kind woman,' Brant murmured, and then he went on into the hotel lobby and up the flight of stairs to his room on the second floor.

He'd had painters working on his cabin while the *Cairo Lady* was tied up, and because he didn't like the smell of paint he'd taken a hotel room for the few days he expected to be in Dakota City.

He hadn't noticed the girl with the parasol since he'd been here, though, and then he remembered that the *River Belle* had tied up that morning, just in from St. Louis. She'd probably come up on the *River Belle* and taken rooms at the Grant. He wondered who she was, and what she was doing in Dakota City, a rough, frontier town, transfer point where the larger, heavier draft lower river boats dropped cargo and passengers to be picked up by the upper Missouri packets bound for Fort Adams, another eighteen hundred miles up the Big Muddy.

In his room he sat down on the edge of the bed, the liquor bottle in his hands, and he thought abstractly about the girl, and then he thought of another lady, the *Cairo Lady*, and he lifted the bottle to his lips.

$$\star \quad \star \quad \star$$

He slept from five o'clock until past ten in the evening, and then he awoke and reached for the bottle on the floor. When he lifted it to his lips only a trickle of brown liquid came into his mouth, and he fired the bottle against the opposite wall.

He stood up, then, his head reeling, his big body swaying. He stood there until he'd steadied himself, and then he walked stiffly toward the door, threw it wide open and went out.

13

The nearest bar was the New Orleans directly across from the hotel. The New Orleans Saloon was frequented by boat captains, officers, boat owners. Deck hands and roustabouts did their drinking in the smaller saloons at the west end of town.

Brant McRae nearly tore the hinges off the New Orleans' doors as he came through. He knocked over a chair as he walked toward the bar. A card player had been sitting in the chair, and he sprawled on the floor when Brant's hip collided with the chair.

The card player cursed, scrambled to his feet quickly as if he intended to make an issue out of the incident, but when he looked into Brant's face he changed his mind, backing away a little, muttering to himself.

They made room for Brant at the bar, plenty of room, and he stood there, both hands resting on the wood, looking at the rows of bottles on the shelves behind the bar. He found himself thinking of the girl with the powder blue eyes and the tiny straw bonnet. She'd been right, of course, and yet she'd been wrong because she did not know all of the circumstances. An eastern girl couldn't know what a river boat meant to a man, not a boat like the *Cairo Lady*.

One of the six New Orleans bartenders slid in front of him, cool, suave, placating. He said, 'What'll it be, Captain McRae?'

Brant stared at him out of those haggard, swollen eyes. His voice still was not muddled; it was not loud, either, but it carried to every part of the big room. He said, 'Mr. McRae, bartender.'

If the bartender had objected pleasantly, Brant would have reached across the bar and driven his fist into the man's smiling face. The bartender, wise in the ways of drunks, nodded instantly. He said politely, 'Of course, Mr. McRae. What'll it be this evening?'

'Whiskey,' Brant said.

He put one elbow on the wood, and he turned to look at the rather silent crowd in the room. He knew many of them, and tonight all of them knew him.

He saw Captain Asa Breen of the packet *Western Star*, an upper river boat, standing down along the bar, a tan, spare man with a beaked nose, thin straight mouth and hard green eyes.

With Breen stood Shelby Flynn, another tall man, the army contractor from Fort Adams upriver, whom Brant had seen once or twice at the post. Flynn was looking at him steadily, calmly, a half-empty liquor glass in his hand. He was dressed in St. Louis clothes, polished boots, black, claw-hammer coat, a pearl gray vest. His ash-blond hair had a slight wave to it, and he had pale blue eyes to go with the hair. His jaws were smooth-shaven, and a slight break in the ridge of the nose was the only flaw in the man. From what Brant knew of him, he had a big supply house across the river from Fort Adams, and the army contracting business to go with it.

Remembering his own poverty, Brant turned and picked up the liquor glass the bartender had slid in front of him. He downed the drink in one long gulp, and it was raw and hot to the stomach, and still it didn't seem to do any good.

When he set the glass back on the wood he saw Shelby Flynn standing in front of him, looking at him steadily. Flynn said quietly, 'Sorry about your boat, McRae. If there's anything I can do, let me know.'

Brant looked at him. Since his boat had burned, not a man had dared mention it to him. A girl had spoken of it but no man, and now for the first time someone had brought the ugly corpse out into the open, and Brant felt better because of it. He'd had this horror in his own mind, and because he could not get it out, it had become magnified a thousand times. He realized now how much better it would have been if he could have sat down with someone immediately after he left the dock and his doomed boat and discussed the matter.

'All right,' Brant mumbled. 'All right, Flynn.'

'Can I buy you a drink?' Flynn asked.

17

Brant shook his head. 'Obliged,' he said.

He knew now that drink was no good; he needed something else to take the devil out of him because liquor could not do it.

Shelby Flynn stepped back, bowing his head slightly, understanding. Brant watched him walk back and say something to Captain Breen, and then Walt Carmody came in. Walt had been first mate on the *Cairo Lady*, and one of the best officers on the upper river. Carmody put a hand on his shoulder and said, 'Why not give it up, Brant? It's no good.'

Brant turned to look at him. Walt had shipped with him on a dozen river boats, and when the *Cairo Lady* had been purchased, Walt was the first man he'd signed aboard. He was a short man, solid in the shoulders, black hair, black eyes, quiet spoken. He wore a seaman's cap and a clean white shirt.

'You're making a fool out of yourself, Brant,' Walt went on, and he was the only man in Dakota City who would dare talk to him like that. 'Sleep it off. You'll feel better in the morning.'

'Jump in the river,' Brant told him.

Walt frowned, and then he shook his head before ordering a drink himself. He said half-aloud, 'We're in for a rough night.'

Brant stood there, his second glass of whiskey in his hand. He looked around the room, at Shelby Flynn who was watching him sympathetically, at Captain Breen, and then at other men in the room, and then he saw the grinning, red-headed Rock Monihan push through the bat-wing doors, and he knew that the gigantic Rock was his man. He knew that even before Monihan came up to the bar.

The Rock had a reputation as a fighting man on the water front. It was said that back east he'd fought professionally with his bare fists, and he'd fought in the back rooms of Dakota City bars for purses or for small bets. He was not, as far as Brant knew, a man who went out of his way to pick a fight, despite his prowess with his fists but he did enjoy fistic engagements, and he was never known to avoid one.

Brant moved down along the bar. He saw Walt Carmody frowning at him as he stepped up to Rock Monihan. The big redhead had a few inches in height, but Brant stood well over six feet, himself, and he weighed one hundred and ninety-five pounds.

Monihan had a flattened nose; his ears were scuffed from many encounters with fists, but his eyes were blue and clear, friendly eyes. He was lifting a glass of liquor to his mouth when he saw Brant standing at his elbow, staring at him intently.

Monihan put the glass down and then turned to face Brant, both elbows resting on the bar, one boot on the bar rail. He knew what was coming. Brant could see that in his eyes. There was a kind of regret in the big redhead's eyes, too, as if he did not relish what lay ahead of him.

Brant said to him, 'Monihan, you have a reputation as a fighting man in this town.'

Rock Monihan nodded. He was smiling a little, almost gracious, as he waited for Brant to pick his fight. Brant stood there, looking like a man who'd just crawled out of a boat's boiler. His clothes were dirty, wrinkled; he'd been sleeping in them. The soot was still on his face and hands. His eyes were red from drink, but he was firm on his feet, and his voice was still clear.

'What is it you want, Captain?' Monihan asked him. Brant McRae's jaw twitched. It was as if they were taunting him with that word, captain. They were laughing at him because he'd lost his boat. He'd been a packet captain for thirty days.

'I am no longer a captain,' Brant said tersely.

'Yes, sir,' Rock Monihan murmured. 'What can I do for you, Mr. McRae?'

'You're a professional fighter,' Brant told him. 'I have a hundred dollars in my pocket says I can whip you.'

Monihan rubbed his jaw with his big hand. He looked down at the floor, and

21

then back at Brant. He'd been at the wharf, and he'd seen the *Cairo Lady* go under. He was a river man, and he knew what Brant was going through. He said softly, 'The liquor no good, Mr. McRae?'

'You want to cover that bet?' Brant countered.

Rock Monihan shook his head. 'Reckon it don't take money to make me fight, Mr. McRae. always obligin'.' He stripped off his coat reluctantly and draped it across the bar, and then he started to tighten his belt. He had thick fore arms and huge fists, but he was not heavy around the middle. Brant took off his coat, also. He handed it to Walt Carmody, and Walt just shook his head in disgust.

'Shall we take it outside, Mr. McRae?' Rock Monihan asked him. 'Kind o' crowded in here.'

Brant nodded. All card games had stopped in the New Orleans bar. Drinkers had come away from the bar and were watching them. There was not too much noise in the place. There were none of the yells, none of the shouts of glee which usually anticipated a fight.

There was no betting, either. They knew why he was fighting; they knew that he had to fight to get the devil out of him. He'd fought flames that afternoon, but a flame is a hard thing to fight. You can't grasp it in your hands; you can't slam your fists into it. It is terrible and deadly and all-consuming, but you cannot fight it, and when it's over you have to fight something or burst. That terrible energy has to be released. The crowd knew it; Rock Monihan knew it, and Brant McRae knew it as he pushed out through the doors of the New Orleans Saloon.

2

The crowd followed them outside, forming a huge ring which stretched from one side of the road to the other. As the word spread rapidly through town, the ring thickened. Men scrambled up on the porch awning above the hotel; they crowded on other porches in the vicinity, They stood on the steps, and they brought up boxes and barrels on which to stand and look over the heads of those in front of them.

Brant McRae walked to the center of the circle and turned around, and waited for Monihan to come down the steps. He saw Captain Asa Breen of the *Western Star*, and Shelby Flynn standing near one of the porch uprights outside the New Orleans bar. Flynn was smoking a cigar, the yellow light from the window close by falling across one side of his face. Rock Monihan came out into the circle, rolling up his sleeves.

He was smiling, cool, a professional fighter, hands held high, head erect, shoulders straight.

Brant said to him, 'Ready?'

When Monihan nodded, he rushed, The devil in him rushed, drove him on with flailing blows which made Rock Monihan retreat in confusion. The red-head had expected him to rush, to put on a wild, furious fight, but he hadn't expected anything as bad as this.

Brant McRae was a wildcat, lashing out with his fists, incredibly fast for a big man, and amazingly accurate for a man who'd consumed a large amount of hard liquor.

Monihan tried to hold him off. He rammed stiff, heavy blows into Brant's face, stopping him momentarily, but Brant came on again, driving his fists at Monihan, striking him on the arms, on the shoulders, on top of the head, on the face, making him give ground. The crowd watched silently.

Monihan slipped as he strove to hold Brant off, and Brant tumbled over him, still swinging. Both men got up, and Monihan shook his head as if to drive the fog out. He was bleeding from the nose and mouth. Brant's right cheekbone had been slashed open, and the blood was dripping off his jaw, reddening his shirt front. Blood trickled from his nose, also, and he could taste it in his mouth, but he was still strong, still fighting, not Monihan, but the devil of bad luck.

Very easily Rock Monihan could have retreated, eluding Brant's wild, vicious blows, and kept retreating, making Brant miss him, but this was not a professional match. There was no money bet on the outcome, and no purse. Monihan fought as a man would fight, straight up, giving as much as he took, retreating only because nothing could hold off the kind of fighter Brant McRae was tonight.

Knowing Monihan, having watched him fight before, Brant had a vast respect for the man even as he battered at his face with his fists, and Monihan smashed at his.

They stood toe to toe on one occasion out in the center of the ring, two big men with iron fists, swinging, and then Monihan went down. He got up immediately, lashed out with his right hand, and Brant fell to his knees.

Brant got up more slowly, but he got up, Monihan watching him calmly, thinking the fight was about over, and then Brant suddenly drove in like a madman, hit Monihan a half dozen times, and Monihan fell into the crowd, carrying three men to the ground with him.

Brant stood there, swaying, face bloody, facing the hotel side of the street, and then he lifted his eyes and he saw the girl he'd seen on the porch steps looking down at him from the window above the porch. She was watching almost calmly, and it was something he did not expect. The light from the hotel windows, all illuminated now, fell full across him, and he realized what a hideous picture he must make.

They'd been fighting steadily for more than ten minutes now, and it wasn't over yet, but at the pace they'd maintained Brant knew it couldn't last much longer. A great weariness came over him very suddenly, and watching Rock Monihan come out of the crowd, steady himself and move forward, he felt the shame of the thing he was doing. All the rage, the bitterness, the pent up emotions he'd felt when his boat burned to the water's edge he was taking out on the hapless Monihan, who in no way was the cause of his misfortune. He was a child tonight, kicking at innocent toys, enraged because a valued toy had been taken away from him.

The fight could not stop now. They were too far into it suddenly to cease fighting, Rock Monihan was grinning, his face a mask of blood, and then he leaped in, swinging both hands, and Brant McRae met him.

Neither man would give ground now. Brant felt as if he were wading through heavy mud up to his neck. He stood there, trying to move forward, a haze coming across his eyes, swinging both hands, feeling them strike, feeling fists strike him.

Once he went down and he got up again, seeing Monihan before him, not much more than a shadow now, and he moved toward that shadow. Monihan must have gone down, also, because he didn't see the man for a while, and he staggered around, looking for him out of eyes which were nearly swollen shut.

Then Monihan apparently got to his feet again. Brant didn't see him, but he felt Rock's blow on the back of his neck, a light blow, the punch of a child, because that was all the dazed, half-blinded Monihan had left.

Brant turned to meet him, and they stood there swinging feebly, tumbling in toward each other, completely exhausted. Brant put his hands on Monihan's shoulders to hold himself up, and then Monihan went down, Brant falling on top of him. They lay there in the road, neither man wanting to get up now.

Monihan mumbled, 'Great fighter, McRae. Buy you a drink.'

Brant shook his head. He reached out, put a hand on Monihan's shoulder, squeezed it, and gasped, 'I'm obliged, Rock.'

Then Walt Carmody and another man hoisted him to his feet. He could not stand up. Carmody got his head underneath Brant's arm and with the help of the other man literally carried Brant to the hotel steps.

Three men lifted Rock Monihan from the dust of the road and carried him into the New Orleans bar, and the crowd started to break up. Walt Carmody was saying grimly, 'Maybe you're happy now, Brant, but you don't look it You'll be sore for a week after this.'

Brant didn't say anything. As they carried him up the stairs to his room, he was thinking of the girl with the honey-colored hair, who'd watched him from the hotel window. He wondered what she was thinking. A fight between river men was always a nauseating affair at best, and the fight he and Monihan had put on would go down as the king of all river fights. In Brant's room, Carmody got him on to a chair, took one look at his face in the light of the lamp, and then said to the man with him, 'Go get Doc Workman. I wouldn't know where to begin here.'

Brant mumbled through his battered, swollen lips, 'Let Workman patch up Monihan first. I'll wait.' Scowling, Carmody got a basin of water and a towel He washed the blood from Brant's face. Brant was beginning to feel the pain of it now. Both eyes were almost swollen shut and he could scarcely see Carmody. He said as the mate worked on him gingerly, 'Notice a new girl in the hotel, Walt? Light hair, looks like an angel.'

'It's a fine time to be thinking of women,' Walt Carmody growled. 'You won't be able to see one with those eyes for a week anyway.'

'She come in on the *River Belle*?' Brant persisted.

'Name of Miss Melodie Wade,' Carmody told him, '*River Belle* brought her up this noon. Understand she's booking passage for the upper river — Fort Adams.'

Brant thought about this. Very few women went up the Missouri to the rough and tumble town of Fort Adams or to the army post across the river from it. Occasionally, the wrong kind of women went up, or an officer's wife or fiancee. He had little doubt that she was of the latter category.

Walt Carmody confirmed this. 'Going up to marry young Lt. Rob Scott,' he explained. 'That's the talk in Dakota City.'

'Lucky man,' Brant murmured. He knew the dashing young Lieutenant Scott of Fort Adams. Young Scott had already made a name for himself in forays against the Sioux on the Dakota plains. 'Who is she booking passage with?' Brant asked.

'Asa Breen's *Western Star*,' Carmody explained, 'is the last boat making the upriver trip this season, now that we're not going.'

Brant McRae didn't say anything to that. The hurt came back, then, but not as bad as it had been. The fight had taken some of the bitterness out of him, and he sat there, silently, thinking about the future.

He was twenty-eight and he'd lost his first boat. Other men had had boats wrecked or burned on them, also. The upper river was strewn with the skeletons of river packets which had either blown up or had their bottoms ripped out by sawyers on hidden reefs.

Even though he was no longer captain of his boat, he was still a licensed pilot, able to operate on the Mississippi or the upper Missouri. The big money for seasoned pilots, of course, was on the upper river. He knew the Big Muddy as few men knew it, and he could make good money, as much as six or seven hundred dollars a trip. Fast packets usually got in two trips from St. Louis to Fort Adams during the summer before the water dropped too low for navigation.

During the winter he could move down the Mississippi and make his runs from Cairo to New Orleans while he waited for the ice to break on the upper river. He would make out well enough, and in years to come he would be in a position to buy another packet.

Doc Workman came in a few minutes later, a small, shriveled man with a goatee and a bald head. Brant said to him before the little man had opened his bag, 'How is Monihan?' The physician looked at him critically before answering, and then he said casually, 'A shade better off than you, I'd say. It was a wicked fight, Mr. McRae.'

Brant nodded. 'I'll make it up to Monihan,' he murmured. 'I forced him into that one, Doc.'

'Feel better now?' Workman asked him.

Brant smiled a little, and it hurt his face when he did so. 'I got it out of me,' he said briefly.

'Sometimes,' Doc Workman answered, 'a fight is a good thing. It may have taken months or years otherwise.'

For fully forty-five minutes the physician worked on Brant's face, cleaning out the cuts, reducing the swellings around his eyes, and when he'd finished he said with a nod of satisfaction, 'You'll be able to see tomorrow, Mr. McRae, but you'll be pretty stiff a lot longer than that.'

Brant nodded. He stretched out on the bed after the physician had gone and he looked at Walt Carmody who was smoking a cigar in the chair across the room. He could feel the tension leaving his body, and it left him completely exhausted. He needed sleep now — hours and hours of sleep to build up the energy he'd thrown away.

Carmody took the cigar from his mouth and stood up. 'I'll drop in tomorrow morning,' he said. 'We'll talk then.'

Brant nodded. 'Obliged for the help, Walt,' he said.

'I'd pick a dog out of the street,' Carmody scowled, and Brant McRae smiled at him, knowing the man, his inherent goodness and gentleness under the hardened exterior.

Brant fell asleep immediately after Carmody closed the door. He didn't sleep well, however, for the first few hours. He had dreams — wild, terrible dreams in which the *Cairo Lady* once more went up in flames and he tried to put the fire out with his bare hands, no water being available. Then he was fighting Rock Monihan again, feeling Monihan's hard, slogging blows to his face. Then someone else entered his dreams — a girl with sky blue eyes and honey-colored hair, a girl with a white dress and a blue parasol, a girl who was heading up to Fort Adams to marry an army officer. That part of the dream Brant McRae did not like either.

3

At high noon the next day Brant came down into the hotel lobby, his face still puffy and swollen, but feeling a lot better than he'd thought be would. He'd slept soundly after the first few hours, and he'd slept late into the morning.

Walt Carmody was sitting in a corner of the lobby, reading an old newspaper, waiting for him, and the first thing Brant said was, 'You know where Monihan holes up?'

'Boardinghouse over on Front Street,' Carmody told him. 'Mrs. Henshaw's.' He looked at Brant critically, and he said, 'How do you feel?'

'I'll live,' Brant murmured. He nodded toward the hotel dining room, and he said, 'Order me a dinner of ham and eggs, Walt. Be back in ten minutes.'

He walked stiffly across the lobby and out into the street. Five minutes later he sat in a chair in Rock Monihan's room, lighting up a cigar, watching Monihan trying to shave.

'Worst part of it,' Brant observed, 'is the shaving.'

'Awful,' Monihan nodded. Like Brant, his face was puffy, discolored, covered with many small cuts.

Brant said to him quietly after he'd gotten the cigar going, 'I'm obliged to you, Rock.'

Monihan turned to grin at him. 'A good fight,' he observed, 'an' no regrets, Brant.'

Brant nodded. 'Anything I can do for you,' he said, 'let me know.'

'Get me a berth on an upriver boat,' Rock Monihan smiled. 'Been dry-docked for two months now, Brant.'

'You're an engineer?' Brant asked him.

'Twelve years on both rivers,' Monihan told him. 'Handled every kind of boat from two to six boiler jobs. Stranded up here when the *Natchez Doll* hit on Shark Rock down below Yankton.'

'See what I can do,' Brant told him.

'Reckon you'll be pilotin' again,' Monihan murmured. 'Always room for good pilots on the upper river. Hear Asa Breen's *Western Star* is takin' on a crew. He might look you up, Brant.'

Brant shrugged. He knew Breen very slightly, a taciturn man who'd come up the Missouri from the lower river less than a year ago. He'd never been on Breen's boat, but the *Western Star* had a good reputation. It was a fast packet, a stern-wheeler, and it could run over mud.

'Breen turned me down,' Monihan said thoughtfully. 'Can't figure that one, either. He's needin' an engineer, an' there's a half-dozen boat captains in this town will give me references.'

Brant McRae thought about that, making nothing out of it. He said, 'Anything I can do for you, Monihan, I'll do it.' Back at the hotel he found his dinner waiting for him, and also two visitors. Captain Asa Breen of the *Western Star* sat at the table with Shelby Flynn and Walt Carmody. Flynn took a look at

Brant's battered face, and then he shook his head commiseratingly.

'Came to ask after your health, McRae,' he said.

Brant looked at him, liking him. He nodded as he sat down, and Captain Breen said, 'We have a business proposition here, Mr. McRae. You can eat while we talk,'

Brant glanced at him, quite sure of what was coming next. Captain Breen was lining up a crew for the *Western Star* which had undergone repairs in Dakota City. He needed a pilot now to take his boat up to Fort Adams.

'The *Western Star* is leaving for Adams in three days,' Asa Breen told him. 'I'm taking on a pilot.'

Brant attacked the platter of ham and eggs, discovering that he was tremendously hungry. He glanced at Walt Carmody, who was listening in, remembering that Walt was out of a job, too, now that the *Cairo Lady* was on the river bottom. Then he looked at Shelby Flynn, wondering what Flynn had to do with this deal. The tall army contractor was smoking a cigar, watching Brant's face and smiling.

'I am wondering,' Asa Breen went on, 'if you'd be interested in taking the *Western Star* up to Fort Adams, Mr. McRae, and then on another shorter trip.'

Brant lifted the coffee cup to his lips, drank the hot beverage, and put the cup down. He said briefly, 'No navigation beyond Adams, Captain. What's the other trip?'

Asa Breen moistened his lips. His green eyes were very intent, and he glanced at Shelby Flynn before speaking. There seemed to be a kind of nervousness running through the man which Brant did not understand. The captain was too tense, too worried.

Breen said slowly, 'I understand you've been up the Yellowstone, Mr. McRae.'

Brant nodded. 'Two years back, piloting a government chartered boat.

Survey work for the Department of the Interior.'

'You went as far as the Big Horn,' Shelby Flynn observed. 'Isn't that true, Mr. McRae?'

Brant looked at him. 'I took the *Lucy Greene* thirty or forty miles up the Big Horn,' he admitted, 'and hell all the way. We had to use our spars every half-mile. The Big Horn is not navigable for river boats, gentlemen.'

'Any trouble on the Yellowstone?' Flynn wanted to know. He was leaning forward slightly, watching Brant's face.

'A rough ride,' Brant shrugged. 'The Yellowstone is not good for commercial navigation. We went as far as the mouth of the Big Horn, and then up the Big Horn a short distance.' Walt Carmody put in quietly, 'That's bad country right now, Mr. Flynn, with Blue Feather uniting the Sioux and the Cheyennes, and the army ready to move in and break it up. I understand they've even been hitting at river boats up near Adams. Big party of them nearly caught the *Eclipse* on her way down through the Sister Island passage.'

'It is bad country,' Flynn admitted. He was sitting back in the chair again, puffing on the cigar, watching Brant, and then he said calmly, 'I have chartered Captain Breen's boat to take me there, Mr. McRae.'

Brant's eyebrows lifted. 'Why?' he asked.

Flynn flicked ash from his cigar. 'A year ago,' he explained, 'I set up a trading post on the Big Horn River. Because of Indian difficulties I think it advisable to abandon the post at this time. There are ten thousand dollars' worth of trade goods on the Big Horn I must either bring out or lose to the Sioux.'

Brant nodded sympathetically. It was a logical reason for the trip. A businessman like Shelby Flynn did not leave ten thousand dollars on a river and forget about it.

'We're paying well for a pilot on this trip,' Captain Breen put in. 'Highest wages on the Missouri — six hundred a month.' ,

Brant toyed with the coffee cup in front of him. 'I'm your man,' he said briefly.

He could appreciate Flynn's predicament. They needed a seasoned river pilot on this dangerous trip into Indian country, and he, Brant McRae, was the only upper river pilot who'd been on the Yellowstone. Also, he wanted to get away; he needed action now to help him forget his disaster. This was more important than the money.

Shelby Flynn put out his hand and Brant shook it. 'Glad to have you with us,' Flynn said.

Brant turned to Captain Breen. He said, 'I understand you are taking on a crew, Captain. I have several good men I'd like to recommend.'

Asa Breen's green eyes narrowed imperceptibly. 'Who are they?' he asked.

'Carmody here was first mate on board my boat,' Brant said. 'I, also, would like to recommend Rock Monihan, the finest engineer on the Missouri.'

Captain Breen's face was expressionless now, but Brant got the queer impression that Breen did not want either Walt or Monihan on the boat this accounting for his hesitation. The captain of the *Western Star* glanced at Shelby Flynn, and Flynn Said promptly, 'By all means, McRae. If you recommend these men they're good enough for us.'

Captain Breen nodded, too, and he pretended an enthusiasm Brant knew he did not feel.

'Good men,' Breen murmured, and Brant was remembering that but a short while before he had turned Rock Monihan down.

Shelby Flynn stood up, shaking Brant's hand again. He said cordially, 'It'll be nice shipping aboard with you, McRae. We are looking forward to a pleasant trip.'

'If the Sioux let us alone,' Brant added dryly.

They all laughed at this remark, and

then Asa Breen and Flynn left. As they went out through the door to the street, Brant saw the girl with the powder blue eyes come in through the door from the hotel lobby. She was all in blue this noon, her pale hair done up in a bunch at the back, and every head in the dining room turned to look as she came in.

Brant half-rose from his chair as she went past and he bowed politely. She recognized him immediately. He was dressed now, having thrown out the ripped, blood-stained shirt, the torn trousers and the scuffed boots. He had on a clean white shirt and a black string tie to go with it. His seaman's cap rested on the table beside him. He was thinking of the name as she came up — Melodie Wade, a hint of the South in it.

Miss Wade greeted him with a pleasant smile as she went past, taking a table at the other end of the room, and Walt Carmody murmured thoughtfully, 'We'll be seeing more of her, Brant, if she's going upriver on the *Western Star*.'

Brant considered that fact, wondering

now how much influence that had had on his signing aboard the *Western Star*. It had not been completely out of his mind when he accepted Captain Breen's proposal.

He was remembering that a river pilot ate with the captain, the officers, and the passengers at the main dining table in the salon. He would have plenty of opportunity to become acquainted with Miss Melodie Wade, and then he remembered that she was engaged to young Lieutenant Scott at Fort Adams.

Chidingly, Walt Carmody said, 'You forgetting Laura, Brant?'

Brant smiled a little. It had been more than two months since he'd seen Laura Graham at Adams. He hadn't been thinking very much about Laura, either, his mind being filled with the purchase of the new boat down in St. Louis, the hiring of the crew, and then the brief trip up to Dakota City.

He was thinking, as he sat at the dinner table, how easily a man could forget about Laura. She was a nice-looking girl, quiet, clean, making dresses for the officers' wives across the river in Fort Adams, well-liked in town, respected at the post. He'd gone to a few dances with Laura; he'd sat in her tiny parlor and chatted with her, but that was all. When he left Adams he also left Laura Graham. He was not in love with her because if he'd been in love he would have missed her downriver, and he did not miss her. He thought about her now as of someone who was far away, and whom he would see eventually, and it would bring him pleasure when he saw her, but he could wait. If that was love it was not the kind of love a man would feel for a girl like Melodie Wade. Brant McRae was quite sure of that.

'Laura,' he said, 'will make some man a good wife.'

'And,' Carmody said thoughtfully, 'she deserves a good man.'

Brant nodded. He pushed his chair back, and he said, we'll pick up Monihan and have a look at Breen's *Western Star*.'

He could forget Laura as quickly as

that. He couldn't forget Melodie Wade, and as they walked toward the door he glanced over his shoulder at her. She was looking straight at him, and he blushed a little.

They found Rock Monihan in the River Man's Restaurant just finishing his third cup of coffee. The big redhead listened as Brant told him of the offer Captain Breen had made.

'Takes a river pilot to get a man a job these days,' Monihan grinned, 'although why he didn't hire me in the first place, I don't know. Breen don't know me from Adam.'

'Shelby Flynn know you?' Brant asked suddenly. Monihan shook his head. 'Everybody knows Flynn on the Missouri,' he said. 'I've seen him an' he's seen me around. We never got together.'

Brant considered that fact, and it didn't make sense. A smart and able captain like Asa Breen should have been highly pleased to sign on a dependable man like Rock Monihan, but still Breen had hesitated, even rejecting Monihan when The Rock, himself, had asked for the job.

They found the *Western Star* at the wharf tied next to the *River Belle*. Brant sat on a barrel top and studied her leisurely. She was a three boiler boat, four hundred and twenty tons, two hundred feet long, a thirty-three foot beam. She could put thirty or forty passengers in her cabins, but on the downriver trip from Adams to St. Louis she'd accommodate two or three hundred Montana miners on her decks.

Twin smokestacks loomed up behind the white pilothouse above the texas deck. There was still some gingerbread work on the rails, and here and there touches of gilt and mahogany, an indication that at one time she'd plied the lower river. Upper Missouri boats dispensed with these frivolities.

Her pilothouse had been sheathed with boiler iron as protection against Indian arrows and bullets, and the tall grasshopper spars were in place at the bow for use when they hit lower water upriver.

She looked fast and sleek, and with a light load, Brant was positive she wouldn't draw more than eighteen inches of water, and she'd make good time.

Walt Carmody, at Brant's side, said thoughtfully, 'Mr. Flynn picked a pretty good river boat for this trip, Brant.'

Brant nodded. 'He'll need a good boat,' he said significantly.

Roustabouts were moving back and forth between the *River Belle* and the *Western Star*, trundling boxes and bales, dropping them down into the hold of the *Western Star*, where a small tram car on miniature tracks rolled them into place.

Captain Breen, and another man with a thin face and yellow hair stood by watching the work, and the thin-faced, hawk-nosed fellow occasionally snapped an order at the roustabouts.

Brant noticed that quite a few of the wooden crates were rectangular in shape, about five feet long, two feet high and two wide. They were very heavy, a windlass lowering them into the hold.

Walt Carmody said, 'What is she taking on, Brant?'

Brant shook his head. The usual cargo up to Fort Adams consisted of staples, mining machinery for the Montana fields, hardware and the thousand and one items a frontier town and an army post would need.

Another man sat on the edge of the wharf, looking at the river, watching the cargo being transferred. He was a small man with a buckskin coat and a gray felt, broad rim hat. Brant took one look at him, and then moved forward, slipping a cigar out of his pocket as he did so.

Monihan and Walt Carmody followed him to the edge of the wharf. The little man on the wharf looked at the cigar Brant waved in front of his nose. Then he took it and slipped it into his pocket. He said briefly, 'Still smokin' Havanas, Brant?'

'Didn't know you were in town, Charlie,' Brant laughed. The last time he'd seen Charlie Barrett, the army scout, was when Barrett rode out of Fort Adams the previous fall with a patrol. Barrett had gone up and down the river with him many times. The mild little man with the child's hands, the smooth shaven face and the soft hazel eyes, was known as the finest scout on the frontier.

'Came down,' Charlie Barrett murmured, 'to see if them dern fools in the States know what's goin' on in the Indian Territory.'

'Do they?' Brant grinned, remembering Barrett's pet peeve.

'Reckon they don't know which way is up.' Barrett scowled. 'Been tryin' to tell Colonel Warburton up at Adams that trouble's going to break loose, an' maybe this summer. Colonel don't believe it. Nobody believes it.'

Walt Carmody said, 'What's the news from Blue Feather, Charlie?'

Charlie Barrett looked at him. 'You wouldn't believe it, neither, mister.'

'I'll listen,' Carmody said seriously.

Brant lighted a cigar and leaned against a wharf post. He wasn't smiling, either. He knew Charlie Barrett, and if Barrett thought there was danger up at Adams it was true.

'Ain't nobody,' Barrett was saying, 'knows how many derned Injuns there are behind them brown hills around Adams. I know. I been out there all winter. Heard the drums poundin' this spring — Sioux, Cheyenne, Arapaho — all united, ready to fight the Army. Blue Feather's the big bear, an' you know how Blue Feather hates the whites.'

'What can they do,' Brant asked, 'against an army post? Colonel Walker has three or four hundred veteran troopers at Adams.'

'Three or four hundred!' Charlie Barrett said scornfully. 'Blue Feather kin bring five thousand across the river any dern time he wants to.'

'Without guns,' Walt Carmody observed, 'without ammunition and without cannon. You can't fight cannon and army Springfields with bows and arrows, Charlie. Blue Feather's smarter than that.'

'An' maybe that's why he's waitin',' Charlie mused. 'Expected him to hit long afore this, but he's waitin', sittin' on his tail.'

Neither Brant nor Walt Carmody said anything. Rock Monihan had stepped aboard the *Western Star* to watch the loading. For a moment all of them watched a windlass lift a heavy, rectangular box into the air, swing it across the wharf, and above the fore-hatch of the *Western Star*.

Charlie Barrett said, 'Nice fire your boat made yesterday, Brant. Who set it?'

Brant looked at him quickly. 'Fire broke out around the stack,' he explained. 'Nobody set it, Charlie, as far as I know.'

The little scout spat into the river. He didn't say anything for a while, and then he said gently, 'Figured they made them new boats better'n that, Brant. *Cairo Lady* wasn't more than three years old, was she?'

'Three,' Brant admitted. He was watching Barrett closely, remembering the little man's almost uncanny intuitive powers. Barrett had lived with the Indians, and he'd developed a sixth sense. It was the first time Brant had really considered the fact that the *Cairo Lady*'s destruction had been anything but accidental. There had been no reason in the world for anyone in Dakota City to burn his boat. He had no enemies as far as he knew. He said slowly, 'What are you talking about, Charlie?'

Barrett shrugged. 'Figured they packed them smokestacks pretty well on the new boats so's fire wouldn't break out. Now if somebody was to take that packin' out you might have a little trouble.'

Brant felt his throat getting dry. 'Why would anybody want to burn my boat, Charlie?' he asked.

Charlie spat into the river. 'Don't know,' he admitted. 'Don't know a lot o' things these days, Brant. Don't know why Blue Feather ain't moved on Fort Adams. She's sittin' up there on the river a thousand miles from nowhere, sittin' like a plum on a tree, ripe an' ready to be plucked, but Blue Feather ain't plucked her. I figured he'd hit in June soon as the mud was dry on the plains an' his ponies could run. Here it is July, an' he's still sittin' an' waitin' fer what?'

Brant smiled. 'Maybe your imagination is running away with you, Charlie,' he said

'Ain't imagination,' Barrett scowled. 'I seen them red devils, an' I know what they kin do. I know Blue Feather, too. He's as smart as any four-star general in the Regular Army.' Captain Asa Breen, seeing Brant, came across the planks and stopped in front of him. He said, 'What do you think of her, McRae?'

'A good boat' Brant nodded. 'What are you carrying, Captain?'

Breen shrugged. 'Mining machinery, staples, trade goods for Mr. Flynn.'

'An' rifle cases,' Charlie murmured,

his hazel eyes watching the windlass hoist another oblong wooden box and lower it into the hold.

'Henry rifles,' Asa Breen told him. 'New consignment Mr. Flynn is taking up to Adams.'

Barrett whistled softly. 'Henrys,' he murmured. 'Didn't know them block-heads back in Washington was givin' our boys anything better than the old Springfields. 'Bout time, though.'

Brant smiled, remembering that that was another of Charlie Barrett's pet peeves. At Fort Adams, and at every army post on the river, the enlisted men were still using the old breech loading, single-shot Springfield rifle, even though for some time traders, frontiersmen and even many Indians were equipped with the new Henry repeating rifle, an infinitely superior weapon.

'Maybe,' Barrett said sarcastically, 'Washington just found out they got a repeatin' rifle on the market. Blue Feather's known that fer two years.'

Brant hardly heard this statement.

Looking up the street toward town he saw Miss Melodie Wade coming toward them, the blue parasol over her head.

He walked toward her as she hesitated on the wharf, and touching the brim of his seaman's cap, he said, 'Coming down to look over the boat, Miss Wade?'

'I thought I'd have a look at my cabin,' Melodie Wade told him, and then she gave him a critical look and added, 'Your face is healing better than I thought it would.'

'Takes time,' Brant smiled. 'Wish you hadn't seen that, ma'am.'

He saw her eyebrows lift slightly, and she said, 'If I'm going to live in this part of the country I'd better get used to such sights. Don't you think so?'

'They're not all as bad as that one,' Brant grinned. 'Monihan is a rough one.'

'You're not a blushing violet, yourself,' Melodie Wade told him. 'Getting used to the fact that you are not a captain of your own boat?'

Brant's jaw tightened. 'A man never gets used to that,' he said dully. 'I am

59

piloting the *Western Star* up to Fort Adams. Anything I can do for you while you are aboard, Miss Wade, I shall consider it a service. I know Lieutenant Scott up at the post.'

'Do you know Rob, really?' she asked, her eyes lighting up.

'I met him in Adams,' Brant nodded, 'I don't know him well.' He wondered how it would feel to have a woman's eyes light up at the mention of his name.

'We became engaged last winter during Rob's furlough,' Melodie said softly. 'I have known him since his graduation from West Point.'

Brant nodded. 'A very fortunate young man,' he murmured.

Miss Wade glanced at him, her eyes twinkling. She said, 'I suppose you have your lady friends along the river, Mr. McRae?'

Brant flushed a little, thinking of Laura Graham. He said evasively, 'Reckon there aren't too many women in this part of the country, ma'am.'

'But you've met those that are,' Miss Wade chuckled. 'Tell me about her?'

Brant was glad to see Captain Breen coming toward them now, and no more was said on the subject. When Asa Breen led Miss Wade aboard, Brant turned back toward town, still intrigued with this eastern girl who could calmly watch a bitter, bloody fight in the dusty street of Dakota City and then say that she expected to become used to it.

4

It was hot and humid on the river Thursday noon. The west bank was half-hidden in a haze, and as usual in this kind of weather the smell of the river came up to the pilothouse, heavy, dank, the river smell which had been in Brant McRae's nostrils for eight long years, and which would never leave him, nor he it.

He had the windows of the pilothouse lowered to benefit by any stray breeze, but even here, high up, there was none. Down below, the last few passengers were coming aboard. A few minutes before Melodie Wade had come across the planks, two colored men bringing her baggage. She'd entered one of the cabins on the cabin deck.

Walt Carmody, as first mate in full charge now, was directing the crew below. Stinson, the yellow-haired second mate, was standing by. Captain Asa

Breen stood on the texas out near the low guardrail, watching the scene, saying nothing. Once he glanced up toward the pilothouse where Brant waited for the crew men to draw the planks aboard and cast off.

The twenty-five or thirty odd passengers making the up river trip were scattered on the texas or down on the main deck. A big crowd from town had come down to watch the *Western Star* depart. They cheered when the last rope was off.

Brant reached up and yanked the bell cord. Down in the engine room be heard the faint tinkle, and then Rock Monihan engaged the heavy pistons. White wood smoke gushed up from the twin stacks; the *Western Star* shuddered a little as she backed away from her berth.

Standing behind the hickory wheel, Brant McRae backed the stern-wheeler out into center river, turned her around and headed up into the current. The Big Muddy boiled down at him, brown with the mud of a thousand tributaries a thousand miles upstream. He felt the force of that powerful current as he edged the packet over toward the west bank.

The big paddle wheel dipped and revolved, the buckets cascading water into the sunshine. Out in center river there was a breeze, and Brant McRae was grateful for it. The cooling breeze blew away the stale smell of Dakota City and of civilization in general. He was glad to be afloat again, even though this was not his boat. He was a river man, a pilot on an upper river packet, and he was proud of his position.

Behind him, seated on the high bench against the pilot housewall, Charlie Barrett said thoughtfully, 'Thousand miles o' mud an' the gateway to the West.'

Brant smiled. Since the Government had closed up the Bozeman Trail overland to the Black Hills and Montana gold fields, practically all traffic was coming up the Missouri. Fort Adams, farthest point of navigation up the Missouri, was the springboard for the Montana fields. Pack trains and wagon outfits rolled from Adams in the spring to Alder Gulch and Virginia City, to Bannock and to Last Chance Gulch. Late summer they returned, a thousand gold-laden miners seeking passage aboard the few river boats which had dared the trip upriver with low water at this season of the year.

An astute packet captain, with a good pilot up above him, could make twentyfive thousand dollars on one trip, cramming his decks with the miners anxious to get back to civilization before the long northwest winter set in. They had the dust to pay for it. Some of the boats had taken down as much as a million dollars in gold on one trip.

Brant McRae had had this late summer trip in mind for the *Cairo Lady*, but it had not materialized. He stood behind the wheel now, pointing the bow of the *Western Star* at Wagonwheel Bluff on the west bank, and then he made a square crossing at the bluff, followed the east bank for a half-dozen miles to

Elbow Bend where he recrossed to the west bank.

The Big Muddy twisted down out of the northwest, laden with trees ripped from the banks along the Yellowstone, the Powder, the Tongue, the Big Horn. Brant steered through the drifting trees; he swung out in center river as they went through the Chute between the Sister Islands, and then he hugged Buffalo Cliff on the west bank where the water was thirty feet deep six feet off the shore.

He knew this river; he knew every foot of it from St. Louis to Dakota City, to Fort Adams; he knew every bend and every twist, every cutoff, every island, and he knew exactly how much water he had in every narrow passageway between the islands. He had to know, or he couldn't have taken the *Western Star* ten miles on this tortuous river with its hundred dangerous reefs; its sand bars and treacherous sawyers, ready to tear the bottom out of a river packet in a matter of seconds. The brown hills unfolded on either side, dotted here and there with clumps of trees, and then, occasionally, darker clumps in the distance which he identified as buffalo.

Charlie Barrett said thoughtfully, 'Shouldn't have no trouble, Brant, till you git past the mouth o' the Powder. Plenty Injuns up above there.'

'You think they'll hit at us?' Brant asked. He watched Melodie Wade come into view, walking up from the after cabins. He saw her stop to talk with Shelby Flynn, who had introduced himself as they came aboard. There were two army wives aboard the *Western Star*, going north to rejoin their husbands at Adams. The other passengers were men — drummers heading up to Fort Adams, a few tradesmen returning to their businesses in town, an occasional lone hunter who'd gone south to see the sights.

'Hard to say,' Barrett told him, 'what an Injun will do. Could be Blue Feather's got 'em all bedded down along the Rosebud or the Tongue, an' then again might be a lot of 'em prowlin', seein' what they kin hit at. A river boat is allus fair game if they kin get a good shot at it.'

'Let's hope they don't get a good shot at us,' Brant murmured, 'not with women aboard.'

'Reckon you're the pilot,' Charlie Barrett observed. 'Steer clear of 'em, Brant.'

Brant smiled. At six o'clock with the sun sinking toward the western hills, Walt Carmody came up to relieve him at the wheel. It was an easy stretch of river ahead, and the mate had spelled him before.

Brant said to him, 'Watch the Hay Island passage. Take it on the east bank, and hug the island. You'll have six feet of water if you let the tree branches scrape your bow.'

'Aye, sir,' Carmody nodded. 'River pretty high yet?'

'Plenty of water,'! Brant told him. 'Can't say how it'll be when we go into the Yellowstone.'

He went downstairs and stepped into the saloon. The passengers had already started to eat, and he found his place at the table with Captain Breen, Flynn, Melodie Wade and the two officers' wives.

Breen introduced Brant to some of the passengers he did not know, and then Brant took his seat next to Miss Wade. Shelby Flynn sat directly opposite them, and he greeted Brant with a warm smile.

'We're making good time, McRae,' he said. 'I understand there's plenty of water in the river.'

Melodie Wade looked mystified. 'Plenty of water in the river?' she repeated.

Both Brant and Flynn laughed.

'The water is still high,' Brant explained. 'In late summer, during the hot months, the water level falls and we have a time getting over some of the sand bars farther north and west.'

The girl nodded. 'It's beautiful, though,' she stated. 'I've enjoyed every minute of the trip thus far.'

Brant saw Shelby Flynn watching her face, and he had his small moment of jealousy, realizing at the same time how foolish this was with Miss Wade engaged to an army officer. 'Buffalo country right now,' Brant told her, 'but some day it will become the greatest farm land in the world. You'll see towns all along the upper Missouri and a thousand barges loaded with wheat and corn. The buffalo will go and there'll be a million head of cattle feeding on that grass.'

Melodie Wade glanced at him curiously. She said slowly, 'You don't sound like the man — ' She paused, groping for the words.

'Like the man who took part in a bloody gutter fight a few days ago?' Brant smiled. 'Reckon I'm ashamed of that now, ma'am'

'What happened to the other man?' Miss Wade wanted to know.

'Engineer on this boat,' Brant explained. 'I got him the job.'

Melodie Wade stared at him. 'But why were you fighting, then?' she asked.

Shelby Flynn explained it. 'Monihan was accommodating Mr. McRae.' He smiled. 'Brant, here, had to blow off some steam.'

Miss Wade shook her head in mock amazement. 'What a strange country,' she chuckled,

'You'll find Fort Adams a little strange, too,' Flynn volunteered. 'It's a new post upriver and pretty raw. You won't have the conveniences and comforts of the East.'

'I shall rise above them,' Melodie Wade said laughingly. There was more small talk, and Brant noticed that Captain Breen took no part in it. The captain of the *Western Star* was at best a taciturn man, and on this trip he seemed to have something on his mind. He had one question to ask Brant and then he lapsed into silence again. He said, 'Are you stopping at Coleman's woodyard tonight, Mr. McRae?'

Brant nodded. Although Breen was captain, when the boat was on the river, the pilot made all the decisions as to the runs and the stops. Coleman's wood-yard was a regular stop-over for river packets, the first stop out of Dakota City. Practically all river boats pulled in at Coleman's for wood the first night out of the river port.

'What is a woodyard?' Melodie Wade wanted to know, 'and what is it doing this far upriver?'

'River boats run on wood,' Brant explained, 'and there are wood hawks all along the river — men who cut wood, pile it along the shore, and then sell it to the first boat pulling in. It's a profitable business, but a dangerous one.'

'Indians?' Miss Wade asked slowly.

'This is Indian country,' Brant told her briefly.

Glancing out the window he noticed that they were running off Tomahawk Bluff on the west bank of the river, and a mile or two north of the Bluff was a bad stretch of river, a series of islands called the Turtles. Walt Carmody wouldn't like to run the Turtles, and by now he'd be looking for Brant up in the pilot house.

Walt greeted Brant as he came in,

'A good boat. She handles nearly as well as the *Cairo Lady*.'

Brant didn't say anything, and the mate stepped away from the wheel, Brant taking it. Carmody watched the river for a few moments in silence, and then he said, 'You take notice of this crew, Brant?'

Brant shook his head. He tilted the cigar toward the ceiling, set the bow of the *Western Star* on a black rock jutting out from the first of the Turtles.

'Look like a bunch of river rats,' Carmody scowled. 'Worst crew I've ever seen on a packet, and I'm surprised at it. Breen has a good boat, and he's been anxious about his officers. Why would he hire the scum of Dakota City on a trip like this?'

Brant thought about that, and it still didn't make sense.

He'd thought at first that Asa Breen and Shelby Flynn were selecting a very special crew to handle the *Western Star* on this trip up the Yellowstone, and now Carmody, who knew crews, marked this one as very inferior.

'Another thing,' Carmody was saying. 'Talking to Charlie Barrett about this post Flynn has up the Yellowstone. Charlie claims he never heard anything about it, but he admits he hasn't been that far west of Adams in a long time.'

Brant scowled. 'What else does Charlie say?' he asked.

'Claims it's a fool idea making a run like that with the Injuns all ready to blow. When you get into the Big Horn it's not more than a hundred or two hundred yards wide, and you'll have to work the spars every mile or two. Sioux will shoot us full of arrows before we're two miles up the Big Horn.'

Brant looked down at the swivel gun on the main deck of the *Western Star*. There was another in the stern which Asa Breen had had installed before they left Dakota City. He'd assumed Breen and Flynn intended to take every precaution on this trip into

Indian Territory, but Charlie Barrett, who knew the Territory, still thought it was bad.

'We'll worry about it,' Brant said, 'when we reach the Big Horn.'

He threaded through the Turtles while Carmody went down to eat, and after he'd passed the last island he came in sight of Coleman's woodyard on the east bank. Coleman's was a cabin where two wood hawks lived — the two Coleman brothers. They had a dozen cords of firewood stacked on a little promontory jutting out into the river.

Sounding his landing bells, Brant turned the nose of the *Western Star* in toward the promontory. In a few minutes they were snubbed to the bank, and the crew men were bringing aboard the firewood.

Brant stepped down to the texas, took a turn around the deck to stretch his legs, and then entered the saloon. It was almost dusk now, and the stars were dotting the sky. Through the window he spotted Charlie Barrett down below, stretched out one one of the woodpiles, smoking a clay pipe.

The ladies had already retired for the evening, but a card game was going on in the saloon. Captain Breen had gone ashore to settle with the wood hawks for the wood. Flynn and three of the other passengers were playing poker at the main dining table.

'Join us,' Flynn invited.

'I'll watch,' Brant said. He had another cigar, and the waiter brought him a brandy. He sat there, sipping the brandy, thinking of Charlie Barrett's remarks, and for the first time wondering about this trip Flynn had scheduled.

The trip up the Big Horn had not appeared so dangerous when Flynn first mentioned it, but that was before Charlie Barrett had told them of Blue Feather and the Sioux-Cheyenne federation. The territory evidently was a powder house ready to be blown sky high. It needed a fuse, and little Barrett, himself, was puzzled as to what would set it off.

Flynn spoke as he shuffled the cards. He said to Brant, 'You've handled the *Western Star* almost a day now, Mr. McCrae. What do you think of her?'

'She'll take us where we're going,' Brant observed, 'if the Sioux let us go there.'

The blond man smiled. 'I'm sure if any pilot can get us through Indian country, you can, Brant. I'm glad you're up in that pilothouse.'

'Your cargo in the hold,' Brant reminded him.

'It's your hair that'll be lost with my cargo,' Flynn grinned. Brant smiled wryly. He said as he looked at his cigar, 'Do you intend to make that trip up the Yellowstone, personally, Mr. Flynn, or are you remaining in Fort Adams when we reach there?'

Flynn looked at him. 'I wouldn't send a boat where I was afraid to go myself.'

'Shouldn't have asked that,' Brant apologized.

'You had a question in your mind,' Flynn said. 'I'm glad you asked it.'

Captain Breen came in, having finished his business with the Coleman brothers. Tom Coleman, a strapping man with a beard, the older of the two brothers, followed him. They had a drink at the bar, Coleman lifting a hand to Brant in greeting. He said, 'Tough about the *Cairo Lady*, Brant.'

Brant nodded, noticing that it wasn't as bad now as it had been. He'd taken a terrible blow, but he was still on his feet, and the day would come when he'd have another river boat registered under his name.

He got up and went out, and he stood on the texas deck with a star-crowded sky over his head, and he breathed the cool night air. A crew man stood guard just aft of the draw plank even though there was no particular need for sentinels tonight. Two hundred miles farther upriver it would be different.

Brant pulled up next to the woodpile on the starboard side of the boat and he stood there for a few moments. Then he heard Charlie Barrett say from the top of the pile, 'Good night fer sleepin', Brant.'

Brant smiled a little. 'It is,' he admitted, but tonight he did not feel like sleeping. He saw the light in Melodie Wade's cabin aft of the pilothouse, and then suddenly he started to think of Laura Graham, quiet, soft-spoken Laura who knew him so well, probably better than any other woman. It would be good to reach Fort Adams and see Laura again even if it was only for a few days. He wondered if she would be glad to see him, or if she thought of him as infrequently as he thought of her. It was a queer thought.

Crossing the planks, he walked along the promontory through waist-high brush until he located the path which led to the Colemans' cabin. He knew Jack Coleman very well and it had been a long time since he'd seen the man.

Moving down the path he came out under the trees about fifty yards from the cabin. He could see the lighted window through the foliage, and then he heard a twig snap softly, and a man called in a low voice, 'Monsieur.'

Spinning around, Brant stared into the shadows. A hulking form seemed to materialize out of thin night air, and Brant said tersely, 'Who is that?'

The man stopped. Brant could see him only dimly. He could make out the wide shoulders, the slouch hat and what looked like a long, buckskin coat. This man had spoken French, but he smelled like an Indian. Brant had seen enough of them around army posts to identify the smell — the diaper smell of unwashed bodies, mingled with the smoke and grease of a thousand campfires; the man who has spent much time with Indians soon acquires the smell himself.

This man in buckskin, who spoke French, had spent much time with Indians. Brant McRae frowned, disgusted with himself that he'd come ashore unarmed. He said again, 'Who is that? Come into the light.'

The big man in the shadows did

not move, and Brant was beginning to sense why. He'd made a mistake here by announcing himself before he was sure of the man he was addressing, and now he had to get away before Brant learned who he was.

Very suddenly Brant was determined to know who the man was, and what he was doing here. There were too many mysteries already about this trip, and he didn't like it.

He took a step forward, not quite sure what he was getting into, and the man in front of him started to retreat. He hadn't uttered a word since he'd first called to Brant, but Brant could hear his heavy breathing. Then very suddenly the man whirled and sprang back toward the darkness of the trees.

He'd taken about three big strides when his foot caught in a tangle of vines. Brant heard him curse as he went down, and then Brant leaped after him, falling on his back as he struggled to get up.

He felt the strength of the man immediately as they wrestled in the undergrowth, and he was wondering if he'd taken on more than he could handle here in the darkness.

They were too far from the boat to be heard on deck unless he lifted his voice and shouted for help, and he couldn't bring himself to do that. The man beneath him was struggling as if to loosen one of his arms, and then as they rolled over, Brant realized what he'd been doing. A knife blade gleamed dully in the night. As it slashed toward him, Brant's left hand whipped out, catching the knife hand, deflecting the knife down.

He didn't know it had entered the man's chest until he felt the strength suddenly go out of his assailant. The man beneath him let out a low moan, the knife hand sliding away from the shaft of the knife, leaving it embedded in his chest.

Brant stood up, scowling. He heard someone coming toward him from the direction of the boat, and then Charlie Barrett's low voice, 'That you, Brant?'

'Come up,' Brant told him. He was

fumbling in his pockets for a sulfur match, and then he found one, bent down and lighted it.

Charlie Barrett came up as he was looking down into a bearded face which was already stiffening in death. The eyes were yellowish; the cheekbones high. He had the long, black hair of an Indian, and a string of colored beads around his neck, inside the buckskin coat.

Brant held the match steady so that Charlie Barrett could see clearly. He said, 'Know him?'

'French Joe LaPorte,' Barrett said succinctly. 'Half-Oglala Sioux, half-French. Lived with the Injuns all his life, though. What in hell is he doin' this far south, an' who put that knife in his chest?'

Brant let the match burn out. He stood up and he stared toward the boat.

'French Joe was supposed to meet someone here,' he said slowly. 'He thought I was the man and then he learned he was wrong. When he ran I went after him. His own knife went into his chest when we scuffled in the brush.'

Charlie Barrett whistled softly. 'French Joe was supposed to meet someone on board the *Western Star*?' he repeated.

'That's how I figure it.' Brant nodded. 'What about French Joe?'

'Not much,' Charlie Barrett murmured, 'exceptin' that he's known all over Injun country as Blue Feather's right hand man. That make sense to you, Brant?'

Brant McRae tossed away the burned out matchstick. He said slowly, 'Not yet, Charlie, but it will.'

5

The *Western Star* pulled away from Coleman's at dawn the next morning, Brant at the wheel. He'd had an early breakfast before the passengers were up.

The morning mist still hung on the river, and it was cool with a promise of heat to come. The Coleman brothers stood on the promontory watching the boat back away. Beyond them was a new mound of earth under which lay the unfortunate French Joe LaPorte.

Brant had taken Captain Asa Breen ashore after the fight, telling him how French Joe had jumped him. He gave no intimation to the *Western Star* captain that he believed the half-breed had been there to meet someone from the boat.

'Robbery,' Breen had said. 'You'd better be careful in the future, Mr. McRae. It'll pay to stay close to the boat.'

'I'll be careful,' Brant told him.

Shelby Flynn was much concerned over the incident, also. He said quietly, 'I'd hate to have anything happen to you, Brant, and not just because you're the pilot aboard this boat and we couldn't get very far without you.'

Brant looked at him steadily. He said, 'Captain Breen thinks it was intended robbery. I have a different theory.'

'What do you mean?' Flynn asked curiously.

'French Joe LaPorte was at Coleman's woodyard to meet someone from this packet,' Brant said flatly. 'I'm positive about that.'

Flynn was staring at him. 'But why?' he asked. 'And who would he possibly want to meet — a breed like that?'

Brant shrugged. 'I don't know,' he confessed. 'There are other queer things about this trip I don't like, either.'

Shelby Flynn scratched his chin thoughtfully. 'Like what?' he asked.

'The crew,' Brant told him. 'Both Carmody and myself label this crew one of the worst we've seen on the river. It looks to me as if Asa Breen scraped the bottom of the barrel to dig them up. River scum if ever I've seen any.'

Flynn was scowling now. 'Why would he do that?' he asked.

'Why,' Brant asked flatly, 'did he turn down Rock Monihan when The Rock asked him for a job on this boat when he needed a good engineer, and Monihan has the reputation as one of the best?'

'I didn't know he'd previously turned down Monihan,' Shelby Flynn muttered. 'That's news to me.'

They stood in the pilothouse, Flynn at Brant's elbow as Brant guided the *Western Star* up past huge drifting cottonwoods, around the tiny islands which dotted this section of the Missouri.

'You think I ought to speak to Captain Breen about it?' Flynn asked dubiously. 'I have a valuable cargo aboard this packet and I don't want to lose it. In addition to my own stock there's a consignment of Henry rifles for the Army. The boys up at Adams will be needing those guns if Blue Feather starts anything.'

'I wouldn't talk to Breen,' Brant advised. 'If he is playing a game of some kind he'd pretend innocence, and then, he'd know we were watching him.'

'So we'll just keep it quiet,' Flynn nodded in agreement, 'and watch Breen. Is that it?'

Brant nodded. He turned the bow of the *Western Star* toward a clump of willows on Sentinel Point, made a square crossing, skirting a very bad sand bar opposite the point, and then followed the west bank.

'How many men can I count on aboard this packet?' Flynn wanted to know, 'in case there is trouble and Breen attempts to steal my cargo.'

Brant stared at the river. 'Carmody, Monihan and myself,' he scowled, 'but how Asa Breen thinks he can steal a cargo and get away with it is beyond me. He's a reputable river captain downriver, and everyone knows you've chartered his boat. If anything happens to you or to the cargo he'll have to explain it.'

Flynn leaned out the window, elbows on the wood. He said over his shoulder, 'Maybe this is all your imagination, Brant. I've always taken Breen to be a good man — maybe a little stiff, but a good man.'

'We'll hope it's that,' Brant nodded.

Flynn straightened up and clapped him on the back. 'Don't worry about it too much,' he laughed.

Down below on the texas they saw Melodie Wade strolling, the blue parasol over her head as protection against the hot sun, and seeing her, Brant frowned again.

'I'll feel better,' he observed, 'when she's safe and sound at Fort Adams. I've never been too anxious to carry women aboard an upper river boat.'

Shelby Flynn was watching the eastern girl, also, and he said with a slight grin, 'She does make matters a little more interesting, though, Brant. Don't you think?'

Brant looked at him, wondering if Flynn felt the same way about Miss Wade as he did.

'A very remarkable girl,' Flynn murmured, 'and a beautiful one. Lieutenant Scott is a fortunate man.

They said no more on the subject, but it was very evident to Brant now that Flynn had taken about as much interest in Melodie Wade as he, himself.

* * *

Two weeks later they passed the mouth of the Yellowstone deep in Indian country. The day before they'd seen a pall of smoke to the west which Charlie Barrett identified as a big Indian encampment. Twice, they spotted Indian riders running buffalo through the barren brown hills off the river.

At the night stops Captain Breen set a heavy guard ashore to watch for possible Indian attacks, but none came. Brant watched the banks carefully as the river narrowed, and a number of times when they had to hug the shore moving through island passages he felt his throat getting dry.

At Drum Island they had to make the passage by the west bank, a heavily wooded bank where a year before a river boat had been hit by the hostiles and nearly taken.

The passengers were sent into the cabins, and the crew crouched behind woodpiles, rifles ready, but nothing happened. They made the passage without any trouble, nothing to disturb the birds singing in the trees, and then Charlie Barrett came up to the pilothouse, shaking his head.

'Figured they'd make one good try at us,' he told Brant. 'That was the place. We'll be in Adams in three-four days.' Brant nodded, He'd been puzzled himself. Moving up the Big Muddy they'd seemed to be immune to Indian attacks. The Sioux had seen them from the shore because no boat could go up the river without the Indians knowing about it, but it was as if they were shutting their eyes.

At noon the next day, as they were moving past Red Flats on the east bank, they heard the sound of firing up the river. Brant had just left the pilothouse for the noonday meal. He stopped on the stairs and listened. Down below on the main deck he saw Charlie Barrett, who'd been sitting in at a card game with some of the deck hands, rise to his feet.

Captain Asa Breen had been talking with some of the passengers on the texas. He, too, stared up the river. It was another hot day, the river streaming in the noonday sun.

Brant watched Walt Carmody steer the *Western Star* around a huge drifting cottonwood, and then head up along the east bank. As he came down to the texas Asa Breen looked at him and said, 'What do you make of it, Mr. McRae?'

The gun firing was continuous, and very clearly Brant defined the heavy bang of army carbines. He said, 'Some of those guns are Springfields. The others sound lighter-rifle cracks. They could be Henrys or Spencers.'

Captain Breen frowned. 'It might be an Indian attack on some of the troopers from Adams.'

Brant nodded. 'Coming from about Skull Cove,' he stated. Charlie Barrett came up the steps to the texas to have a better look up the river. The little scout glanced at Brant, and then shook his head. 'Trouble,' he murmured.

'Indian rifles?' Brant asked him.

Barrett smiled faintly. 'Ain't no other kind o' rifles,' he observed, 'would be shootin' back at army carbines up in this country, Brant. I don't like it. Too derned many o' them rifles to suit me.'

Brant had noticed that, too. The crackle of rifles seemed to be much heavier than the banging of the army guns.

'Could be,' Charlie Barrett said, 'derned Injuns have holed up some o' our boys along the river. Maybe a scout patrol the colonel sent out.'

'Coming from the west bank,' Brant told him, 'about up near Skull Cove.'

Charlie Barrett glanced up at the pilothouse, 'Feel better if we had a man up there knew the river, Brant. We might be runnin' into somethin' here. If army troops are stuck along the river they'll be needin' these swivel guns Asa Breen's mounted on his boat.'

Brant had thought of that, too. As he started up the steps to the pilothouse he saw Melodie Wade come out with Shelby Flynn and several other passengers. They, too, had heard the sound of firing.

Walt Carmody said when Brant came in, 'Trouble.'

'Had to come sooner or later,' Brant murmured. 'We've been lucky, Walt.'

He took over the wheel, Carmody going below for further orders from Captain Breen, and then Charlie Barrett came into the pilothouse, whistling softly. He stood by the open window, looking out, watching the river.

'What's ahead?' he asked.

'Bell Island,' Brant told him, 'and then Snake Bend. Skull Cove is a mile or so north of the Bend . . .

Barrett didn't say anything as Brant moved the *Western Star* past the east side of Bell Island, a tiny, wooded islet in center river. As they passed the north end of the island, the scout said, 'River pretty wide up ahead?'

'Five hundred yards and more,' Brant told him.

Down below on the texas Brant saw Shelby Flynn look up at him. He'd rung his bells for full speed ahead, and Rock Monihan was complying down in the engine room.

The gun firing had slackened off now, and they could only hear occasional shots. It was quiet for nearly ten minutes as the *Western Star* steamed up the river, and then it broke out again, heavier than before.

Charlie Barrett scowled and spat through the open window. 'Clear as a windowpane,' he muttered. 'Sioux have some o' our boys holed up on the west bank. Must be a hell of a lot of 'em, and only a small patrol of ours. Our boys probably fought 'em off, an' now they're chargin' again. Hope they kin hold out.'

Captain Breen had been talking with Flynn, and now Brant saw him turn and start up the stairs to the pilot-house. A moment later he came into the room. The *Western Star* was swinging around Snake Bend, and as they came into open water Brant saw the opening through the barren hills. This was Skull Cove, once a part of the river, the main stream. The Big Muddy had changed its course, finding a new cutoff. Debris had blocked up the north entrance of Skull Cove, but it still ran a mile or so into the hills. Occasionally, when the river was high, packets pulled into the cove for the night stop. A sand bar had formed across the entrance to the cove, and it was impossible to enter unless the water was quite high.

It wasn't high enough now. Brant McRae knew that very definitely. He'd been watching the watermarks along the shore for miles, and in the past few weeks the river had dropped sharply, which was to be expected this season of the year. It would keep falling all summer, and it would not rise again until the following spring when melting snow from the mountaintops sent the water rushing down a thousand freshets. 'Comin' from Skull Cove,' Charlie Barrett said. 'That fight's up along the cove.'

Brant glanced at Asa Breen who stood at his elbow. In a situation like this it was up to the captain to make the decisions. If the besieged troopers needed the aid of his small cannon he had to decide whether they'd move in. If the fight, of course, was at the other end of the cove, or out of range of their cannon, it was out of the question.

Asa Breen said, 'Pull up near the cove, Mr. McRae. We'll have a look into it.'

Brant just nodded. They could hear the distant yelling of the Indians now, interspersed with the crackle of rifles and the bang of the heavier army weapons.

Brant noticed gloomily that not as many Springfields seemed to be firing.

Charlie Barrett had noticed that, too, and he scowled as he stared intently at the cove. Captain Breen said, 'Can you enter that cove, Mr. McRae?'

'No,' Brant told him. 'We won't have two feet of water above that bar across the entrance. The *Western Star* needs at least three feet with this load.'

Asa Breen didn't say anything. Brant sounded his bells for half-speed, and they moved cautiously up toward the cove. Down below on the texas every passenger aboard the packet watched silently, listening to the guns, to the shrill, triumphant yells of the Sioux.

A hill blocked out their view until they were nearly abreast of the cove, and then they saw it. Brant heard Charlie Barrett's quick intake of breath. He spun the tiller wheel, keeping the *Western Star* off the bar which lay about fifty yards ahead of them. They crept up along the bar, the engines keeping the bow into the current.

On a ridge on the north bank of the cove about a half-mile up the cove lay the army detail. Brant could see the men in blue firing from behind dead horses and tiny breastworks they'd scooped from the earth. They'd picked a good spot for their stand, the highest ridge in the vicinity, but they weren't going to hold it long.

Brant took one look at the horde of Indians swinging around the ridge, firing as they rode, and he knew it was only a matter of time before they swept over the ridge.

'Four or five hundred Sioux,' Charlie Barrett growled. 'Ain't more than fifty o' our boys on that ridge, an' a lot of 'em dead an' wounded already.'

The troopers had seen the *Western Star* edging up toward the cove, and thinking it was coming to their assistance with its small cannon, they set up a faint cheer.

Brant McRae started to feel sick. The sweat broke out on his hands as he gripped the tiller wheel, and he studied the cove opening desperately, even though he knew the bar extended from bank to bank, and it was utterly impossible to get in.

'Reckon if we got in there close enough,' Charlie Barrett muttered, 'an' let them Sioux have a few cannon balls drop among 'em, they might ride off. We could pick up that detail an' take it up to the fort.'

'We can't get in,' Brant said thickly. 'I know that bar. If we try it we'll stick and they'd have us, too.'

He glanced down at the three women on the deck. Melodie Wade was standing next to Shelby Flynn, hypnotized by the sight.

Asa Breen said slowly, 'You think it would be a bad risk trying to get in there, Mr. McRae?'

'Not a risk,' Brant growled, 'an impossibility. You can't run a river boat over mud.'

'How about your spars?' Charlie Barrett asked him, still watching the wild-riding Sioux swing up toward the ridge, fire, and then speed away again.

'Spars are no good here,' Brant told him. 'There's deep water on the other side of the sand bar. We'd have nothing to dig our spars into.'

The Sioux had spotted the packet on the outside of the cove, and about fifty of them were speeding up along the shore, yelling, brandishing rifles.

They stopped before they were within rifle shot, held a short conference which Brant and Charlie Barrett watched curiously, and then rode back to the scene of the fight.

The troopers had stopped firing, and they were watching the river boat, waiting for it to come into the cove with its cannon. Brant stood at the wheel, his face set in tight lines, a chill in his heart, knowing that he couldn't do a thing to help. There were thirty-five men aboard the *Western Star*, but sending them ashore would be tantamount to suicide. Only the cannon could help, but they couldn't get the cannon near the besieged troopers.

Shelby Flynn stepped into the pilot-house, jaws set grimly. He said to Brant, 'Can we get them out?'

Brant was racking his brain for a possible solution, knowing that there was none. He said dully, 'Big sand bar across the mouth of that cove, Flynn. We can't get in.'

Flynn was staring at him. 'We can't get in?' he repeated. 'Those men are doomed, Brant!' Brant didn't say anything. He was watching the troopers on the ridge, knowing what was going on in their minds. They were expecting rescue, and he wasn't coming in for them. He was leaving them to die.

'Can we take a chance?' Flynn asked wildly. 'To hell with the cargo.'

'We have women aboard.' Brant almost snarled. 'We can't get over that bar, Flynn, and if we stick, this boat will be taken. The Sioux will hit at us from all sides and the cannon won't help.

There's nothing Indians like better than to capture a river boat.'

'With women aboard,' Charlie Barrett added significantly, 'an' I say git them women out o' sight. If the Injuns see 'em they'll go wild.'

Captain Breen called down the order for the women passengers to remain in their cabins. Brant saw Melodie Wade glance up at him as she moved toward her cabin, and he noticed that her face was pale. This was her first glimpse of the Sioux in action, and it was not a pleasant one. She'd seen the difference in numbers, and she realized how bad it was for the troopers. She, too, was expecting him to support the men in blue.

'This is terrible,' Shelby Flynn was muttering. 'We can't let this happen.'

Brant's hands were sweating as he gripped the wheel. The big paddle wheel revolved slowly, keeping them abreast of the cove entrance. For one long moment he wondered if he ought to take the chance, risk the run over the bar and if they did stick fast hope that they could fight off the Sioux attack.

Against those hundreds of wild red riders he realized how ridiculous this would be. If they stuck they were doomed, and the *Western Star* would stick. He knew this bar; on a previous trip he'd had leadsmen go out in small boats to measure the depth as he contemplated making a night stop there. He knew exactly how much water he had over the bar at this season of the year, and he knew that he could not go over.

'Be comin' pretty soon,' Charlie Barrett murmured. 'Red-skins are linin' up fer another charge.' They stared silently at that little band of men in blue entrenched on the ridge, men who were doomed to die in a very few minutes. Brant happened to glance at Asa Breen to his left and he saw something in the man's face which astonished him. He'd assumed the taciturn, emotionless Breen would take this better than any of the others, but Captain Breen was upset the way Brant had seen few men upset. Sweat poured down his face; his green eyes were wild, horror-stricken, and a pulse was pounding in his temple. His lower jaw sagged and he was trembling a little.

Barrett said slowly, 'Be a lot of 'em blamin' you fer this Brant. I'm takin' your word for it that you can't get in there.'

A guidon hung limp from the pole which had been planted in the center of the army perimeter. At three o'clock in the afternoon, this bright, cloudless July day, the heat was searing. Brant could imagine how it was up on that ridge where the men in blue waited for another Sioux charge. The hostiles had drawn back for another conference, and Brant could hear them yipping excitedly. They were out of gunshot of the ridge, and Brant saw one of the men in blue get up from the ground and walk a few yards in the direction of the river. He stopped and he stared at the boat, hands on hips, hatless, a white bandage around his head. It was as if the man were berating the captain, crew and especially the pilot for their cowardly refusal to come into the cove. From the standpoint of the troopers there was no danger for the boat. Staying out in the middle of the cove they could send their shots from the cannon among the Sioux, and the hostiles in turn could do very little damage to them. It was a long rifle shot from the shore to the boat.

'Here they come,' Charlie Barrett murmured.

Brant closed his eyes and then opened them again. The Sioux charge had started, and it was a terrible, awe inspiring sight. Five hundred hideously painted riders, stripped almost naked, glued to their sturdy little mounts, charged up the slope, firing as they came, every one of them yelling like a fiend from hell.

White puffs of smoke lifted from the trooper barricade, pitifully small compared to the volume of fire coming from the Sioux guns. Watching, Brant figured there weren't more than twenty or twenty-five able men firing their

Springfields. But they kept firing, even with the lead Sioux riders less than twenty five yards away, coming on in a huge multicolored wave. The men in blue held their ground, worked the bolts on their Springfields and sent rider after rider to the ground.

It was over in another moment.

The red wave had gone over the spot of blue on the ridge.

There was a cloud of dust around the guidon, and then it disappeared. Still more and more Sioux were coming up, some of them dashing full into the dust cloud, others dismounting, racing forward with sharp-pointed spear or rifle. The yelling was sickening.

Reaching up with his right hand, Brant McRae pulled the bell cord. When the big paddle wheel started to revolve with force again, he spun the tiller, turning the *Western Star* away from the cove, heading across the river. He did so without orders from Captain Breen. Asa Breen was watching the massacre through the open window, standing very stiff, very straight. He hadn't said anything, and Brant could see that he'd regained control of himself.

Charlie Barrett was lighting his clay pipe, leaning out the window as he stared at the other shore. Brant noticed that his brown hands trembled a little, but his voice was cool, calm. 'Quite a business,' Charlie said. 'You figure on tyin' up over there, Brant?' Brant nodded.

Charlie Barrett continued. 'Take 'em an hour or two to git finished back there. Good thing there ain't any squaws with 'em. The squaws are worse'n the bucks when it comes to workin' over prisoners an' dead men.'

Captain Asa Breen opened the door and went below. Brant sounded his landing bells, and the *Western Star* edged in toward the opposite shore. Two crew men went over the side with ropes, and in a few moments the packet was snubbed into the bank.

Brant stepped back from the wheel and sat down on the bench against the wall. In the distance he could still hear the triumphant yells of the victorious Sioux.

Charlie Barrett said sympathetically, 'Go down an' get yourself a drink, Brant. Looks like you need it.'

Brant shook his head miserably. He watched Walt Carmody come into the pilothouse, and Walt put a hand on his shoulder, knowing what he was going through.

'Army's fault,' Carmody scowled. 'They shouldn't be sending small patrols into the hills with thousands of Sioux and Cheyenne riders on the prowl.'

'Trouble is,' Charlie Barrett said, 'none of 'em believe Blue Feather is that strong. Army figures it's fightin' a few hostile tribes who won't come in to the reservations. This might be the last big stand the Sioux make, an' there'll be hell to pay afore they're finished.'

Walt said to Brant, 'You made the right decision, Brant. They might blame you at Adams, but even if we could have gotten the *Western Star* into the cove, we couldn't be sure the Sioux would have run from a few cannon balls.'

It was very quiet aboard the Western Star as they crossed the Missouri, two hundred yards wide at this point. Brant went downstairs after the packet was snubbed into the bank. He didn't see Melodie Wade nor the other women passengers, but he heard one woman crying hysterically in her cabin.

Shelby Flynn and Captain Breen were in the saloon when Brant entered, and Flynn had been speaking with the captain. He turned around now, shaking his head, pushing a bottle toward Brant.

Breen, his face a strange, mottled color, looked at Brant and then looked away. Brant poured himself a stiff drink and downed it.

'A rotten business,' Flynn muttered.

Brant pushed the glass away and went out on the deck. He saw Melodie Wade coming from her cabin, walking toward him. He waited for her under the canvas awning which had been stretched over part of the texas as protection from the sun. She said slowly, 'Is it all over, Mr. McRae?'

'It's over,' Brant said, He didn't look at her. 'And they're all dead?' Miss Wade murmured.

Brant nodded. He ran a hand across his face, glad that they were far enough away now that they could no longer hear those triumphant, bloodthirsty yells.

'There was no way to save them, Mr. McRae?' the girl asked quietly.

Brant looked at her now. 'If it would have helped,' he said tersely, 'I'd have gone ashore with a knife. Those men were doomed before the *Western Star* came in sight.'

'I believe you,' Melodie Wade told him softly. 'No matter what others may think, I believe you, Mr. McRae.'

Brant moistened his lips. 'I'm obliged,' he said.

'Those men were from Fort Adams?' she asked.

'Only post around here,' Brant nodded. 'A small patrol sent out by the commanding officer to ascertain the strength of the hostiles, or — ' He stopped because Melodie Wade was looking at him strangely, and then he remembered, and a chill went through him. Lt. Rob Scott, the man to whom this girl was engaged, served at Fort Adams!

6

At Six O'clock that evening, an hour after the noise had died down across the river, and as they were preparing to cast off and return to the other shore, they heard a bugle. A cloud of dust was moving down from the north toward Skull Cove.

Charlie Barrett said dryly, 'Reinforcements comin' from the fort. Gettin' there just in time to bury the dead.'

Brant backed the Western Star out into midstream, swung her around, and headed for the other shore. They could see the column of troopers moving through the brown hills several miles away. They were riding fast.

Captain Asa Breen stood in the pilot-house as Brant pointed the *Western Star* in the direction of the cove. He said quietly, 'We'll tie up over there, Mr. McRae. I'll have to talk with the commanding officer in charge of that relief column.'

Brant nodded. There was still plenty of light, but the sun was low in the sky. The heat of the day had abated, and a cooling breeze moved down the river as they crossed.

From the pilothouse they watched the relief column approach the ridge of death on which the small detail had made its heroic stand. Brant blew his whistle twice before nosing in toward the bank. He went ashore with Asa Breen, Charlie Barrett and a score of other passengers. They had to walk the distance from the head of the cove back to the ridge, and Brant brought up the rear, walking slowly, not liking to think what they would find up on that ridge.

The troopers from the relief column were there gathering up the greenbacks which were scattered across the ridge. They were walking about solemnly, faces grim, picking money from the grass, turning it over to a hard-faced, hard-eyed first sergeant.

Charlie Barrett said to Brant, 'Pay day a week ago back in Adams. Reckon these boys didn't have time to spend much of it when they were called out on this detail. They ain't spendin' it now, either.'

Brant nodded. The Sioux had scattered the worthless pieces of green paper all over the brown grass of the ridge. They'd taken everything else, however. The stripped, white bodies of the dead troopers were sprawled on the grass in an area comprising about half an acre. They'd been worked over with arrows, lances, knives.

The first of the *Western Star*'s passengers, a round-faced flaxen-haired little drummer from St. Louis came running up, took one look, and then fainted.

Charlie Barrett said succinctly, 'Ain't as bad as I've seen it sometimes. You should see 'em after the squaws get finished with 'em. This band had no women with 'em.'

Capt. Mason Wilks was in charge of the relief column, two hundred troopers from Fort Adams. He was a tall, spare man as straight as a ramrod, with bleak blue eyes. Brant knew him slightly.

'A messenger came in to Adams two days ago,' Captain Wilks explained to Asa Breen. 'The detail has been holed up here as long as that. We've been moving eighteen hours a day to get here.'

'You were three hours late,' Breen told him.

Captain Wilks looked at him steadily. 'You saw it?' he asked.

Captain Breen nodded. 'Couldn't get our boat into that cove to help with our cannon. Mr. McRae said it couldn't be done.'

Mason Wilks turned to look at Brant. He nodded slightly, almost curtly, but he didn't say anything, and Brant knew what he was thinking. When men's lives were in danger the impossible had to be accomplished some way. That was the army way of thinking, of acting.

Breen was saying, 'Who had charge of the detail, Captain Wilks?'

Mason Wilks acted as if he'd just thought of something. He looked at Brant strangely, a bitter smile coming to the corners of his mouth. He said slowly, 'A friend of Mr. McRae's.'

'Who?' Brant asked quickly.

'Lt. Robert Scott,' Captain Wilks told him. 'He was hard to recognize.'

Brant looked at him, and then turned and started to walk back toward the boat. He heard Asa Breen say, 'We have Lieutenant Scott's fiancee aboard my boat, Captain Wilks.'

He didn't go back to the boat. He went upriver a short distance, and he was sitting on a rock overlooking the water when Charlie Barrett came up, puffing on his clay pipe.

'Bad business,' Charlie scowled as he sat down on the ground. 'Young Scott was a good soldier.'

Brant didn't say anything. He sat there, his heart dead within him, staring at the river.

'Reckon young Scott knew what he was gittin' into when he entered West Point an' then came out here, Brant. Soldierin' kin be pretty tough sometimes.'

Brant rubbed bis hands together. He didn't say anything, and he was thinking of Melodie Wade. She was courageous, but this was more than a girl could take.

'Captain Breen told her,' Charlie Barrett murmured. 'She didn't break to pieces, but she's hard hit. She'll git over it, Brant. I seen 'em git over things before. This ain't a nice country. Maybe it will be some day, but it ain't now.'

She'll hate me, Brant thought, she'll hate every breath I take from now on. She'll regret each day that I'm alive and he's dead.

'Have to go back some time,' Charlie Barrett said.

Brant got up. He walked back to the boat and went aboard. The burying detail was just coming back, hot, sweating, dirty. They looked at him as he crossed the planks, and one soldier cursed under his breath.

★　★　★

It was high noon the next day when Miss Wade came out of her cabin. She'd had no breakfast that morning, nor had she eaten the previous night as far as Brant knew, but she had complete command of herself as she stepped into the dining room.

She included Brant in the faint smile she gave to the men when they bowed to her. There was little talk at the table, and when the meal was over Brant stepped outside immediately. He was standing with his back to the saloon, looking upriver, when he heard a light step behind him, and then Melodie Wade said quietly, 'Mr. McRae.'

Brant turned around. She was looking at him steadily, and there was no accusation in her eyes. She said evenly, 'I told you yesterday, Mr. McRae, that no matter what happened I would accept your statement that you couldn't help those besieged men.'

Brant moistened his lips. 'I know,' he murmured.

'I still feel the same way,' Melodie

119

Wade told him simply. 'Rob died bravely, facing the enemy. A soldier would have wanted no better death. I do not hold you responsible for his dying, Mr. McRae.'

Brant just looked at her. There were no words to be said at this time. He just nodded, and then Walt Carmody came over to express his sympathy, and as Brant listened to him he noticed something else. Walt was very much interested in the girl, and it was not a casual interest. This came to him as a distinct surprise. He'd seen Walt watching Melodie Wade on occasion, and now he realized that the mate was definitely aware of Miss Wade's charms, and possibly even in love with her! This fact was vaguely disturbing to Brant who had never seen Walt take an interest in a woman before. The stolid, honest, dependable Walt Carmody was the kind who loved one woman in his life, and then never again.

During the next two days, finishing the run up to Fort Adams, Brant watched the mate carefully, noticing the difference in the man. Walt had become strangely silent, but when ever Melodie Wade came in sight he brightened up immediately.

Shelby Flynn, however, commanded most of Miss Wade's attentions. Flynn, as a passenger aboard, had more time, and quite often Brant watched them from the pilothouse as they sat under the canvas awning on the texas, talking.

Walt Carmody watched them, too, and Brant knew that the mate was tearing himself apart with jealousy. Walt said once as they were changing positions, Walt taking the wheel for an hour, 'You think Flynn is in love with Miss Wade, Brant?'

Brant shrugged. 'Hard to say,' he murmured, and he wasn't sure but that he was in love with Miss Wade, himself, making it a queer, triangular affair because he liked both Walt and Flynn.

'Whether he is or not,' Walt scowled, 'he has the inside track.'

Brant didn't say anything to that.

The *Western Star* docked at the wharf at the town of Fort Adams late in the afternoon of the second day after the cavalry massacre.

Fort Adams, the army post, was on the west bank of the river, the town being on the east bank. Brant, following Captain Breen's instructions, docked on the town side to unload some of Shelby Flynn's cargo, and then to take on supplies for the trip up the Yellowstone.

The town of Fort Adams sprawled along the water front, extending back two blocks. It was a collection of ramshackle log and board buildings, straggling unevenly up and down a long main street which faced on the water, and then over? flowing into the two smaller streets.

Flynn's big warehouse lay at the south end of town, a low frame building with a big wagon yard and ox corrals in the rear. When Brant raised the question as to the army cargo of rifles, Captain Breen said briefly, 'We'll ferry them across to the post immediately we tie up. Mr. Flynn asked that we tie up on the town side.'

In the pilothouse Brant smoked a cigar as the crew men were tying up below, throwing the planks across to the wharf. Walt Carmody stepped into the room, smiling a little and he said, 'We made it this far, Brant, and no trouble, aside from that affair in Skull Cove.'

Brant didn't say anything. A crowd had come down to the wharf to watch the *Western Star* tie up, and it was a silent crowd, many of them staring up at the pilothouse.

Carmody said grimly, 'Captain Wilkes got the news back here about the massacre, Brant. Rider got in this morning.'

Brant nodded. 'I won't be a very popular man in this town,' he said bitterly.

'It'll blow over,' Carmody assured him. 'Let's go ashore and have a drink.'

Brant looked at him in surprise. 'You taking that cargo off?' he asked.

Walt Carmody shook his head and grinned. 'Captain Breen said Stinson could take care of it. I have the afternoon and evening off. Not a bad man, Breen, when you get to know him.'

Brant McRae didn't know Asa Breen. He'd gotten the impression during the trip upriver that Captain Breen was a man laboring under a terrific burden. Breen was tight-lipped, almost bleak, saying very little to anyone. He had little to do with the handling of the boat once it was under way, Brant making the decisions as to when they should start, how long they would run, and where they would pull up for the night. That was always the pilot's business. The two mates handled the crews, giving Asa Breen plenty of time for his thoughts, which were deep and not always pleasant. Brant could see that from his face.

The *Western Star* captain was talking with second mate Stinson as Brant and Walt Carmody crossed the planks, Brant noticed that Breen watched them go even as he spoke with the yellow-haired Stinson.

Rock Monihan was waiting ashore for them, having banked his fires for the night. He said to Brant with a grin,

'Got a powerful thirst on, Brant. You joining me?'

'For one,' Brant smiled. 'Careful in this town, Rock. It's rough. You might find yourself in an alley before the night's over, with your pockets picked and a knife in your back.'

'A tough town,' Monihan chuckled, 'for a tough man.' They passed through the silent, grim-faced crowd at the wharf, and as they were going through, Brant heard a big, black-whiskered man with a teamster's slouch hat and high boots say sourly. 'That's him. Let forty-two good army boys go under. Afraid to take his boat — '

That was all he had time to say. Brant McRae slashed through the crowd, his vision blurred. He grasped the big, be-whiskered man by the coat lapels, jerked him around, and then lashed out with his right fist.

He heard the bones crack in the teamster's face as he went down, the left side of his face peculiarly twisted out of shape. Stunned, his mouth working, the teamster tried to rise to his feet, but that terrible, hammer-like blow had crushed him.

A man behind Brant said, 'Jaw's broken. He ain't fightin' anybody for a hell of a long time.'

The teamster lay there, shaking his head, unable to get up. He stared at Brant stupidly. At Brant's elbow Rock Monihan said softly, 'Glad I ain't fightin' you today, Brant. Reckon you're loaded fer bear.'

Brant started to push through the crowd again, face white, drawn, bitterness in his eyes, and then he heard a woman say softly, 'Still knocking men down, Brant?'

Brant McRae whirled. Some of the tightness left his face. He looked into a pair of cool gray eyes, very calm eyes which studied him thoughtfully. The face was not beautiful as Melodie Wade's face was beautiful, but it was a fine face, the features well-shaped and framed by a soft mass of chestnut brown hair. She was hatless as she stood in the sunshine among the crowd on the wharf, and her face was tanned, which was very unusual for a woman.

Brant said slowly, 'Laura. How are you?'

'Glad to see you,' Laura Graham told him, 'but not fighting again. Aren't you ever going to control that temper, Brant?'

Brant looked around at the grinning Rock Monihan. He said, 'Rock, will you look after that fellow. Get a doctor for him and put him up in a good room at my expense.'

'Sure,' Monihan nodded.

Walt Carmody touched his. hat to Laura Graham, smiled and said, 'See you around the Riverman's Bar, Brant.'

He walked off, and Brant took Laura Graham's arm, steering her through the crowd.

Laura said, 'And still picking up the pieces after your fights, aren't you.'

'He made a remark,' Brant scowled. 'I didn't like it.'

'I heard it,' Laura nodded. 'It wasn't nice.'

Brant's lips tightened as they stepped up on the board walk and headed north along Grant Street toward the little dress shop Laura Graham maintained.

'What are they saying in this town?' he asked tersely.

'It's not complimentary,' Laura murmured. 'The news only reached Fort Adams this morning. It seems they put a lot of the blame on you, Brant.'

'I couldn't take a boat into that cove,' Brant grated. 'I'm a river pilot, I know what a boat can do and what it can't do. The *Western Star* couldn't get into Skull Cove. She'd have grounded and the Sioux would have wiped us out, too, in no time. We had women aboard.'

'I saw one of them come ashore,' Laura Graham observed blandly. 'Very pretty, too.'

'She was engaged to Lieutenant Scott,' Brant muttered, 'who was in command of that detail the Sioux wiped out.'

Laura Graham stopped on the walk. She looked up into Brant's face, and she said, 'I'm terribly sorry.'

'Hard thing to take,' Brant scowled.

They walked along, passing bar after bar, Brant noticing that the town was more crowded than he'd ever seen it before. Swarms of miners, apparently just in from the mine fields, roamed the streets or lounged in front of the many saloons.

'I heard about your boat,' Laura said quietly. 'I'm very sorry about that, too, Brant.'

Brant bit his lips. 'She was a beauty,' he murmured. 'I was bringing her up to Adams this summer. Figured you might be going downriver this fall and you'd ride on the *Cairo Lady*.'

He glanced down at her as they walked, thinking how strange it was that he hadn't thought too much about Laura Graham in the three months he'd been downriver. They'd been friendly for two years now. He'd had many a cup of coffee in the back room of her shop, and many a pleasant chat, but when a girl like Melodie Wade came along he'd permitted

Laura Graham to slip into the background, which was a very foolish thing to do because Laura could have had any one of a dozen good men in town.

'You'll have another boat,' Laura told him calmly. 'You're known as the best pilot on the upper river. You can almost make your own price on any boat you handle.'

'I'm taking the *Western Star* up the Yellowstone in a week or so,' Brant told her. 'Shelby Flynn's chartered the boat to bring out supplies from a trading post he is abandoning on the Big Horn.'

They were in front of the dress shop now, and Brant held open the door for her. They went in, walking to the little back room where Laura put the water kettle on the stove. She said then, 'That's dangerous country, isn't it, Brant, the way things are this summer?'

Brant shrugged. He watched her moving around the room, putting ground coffee into the pot, setting out cups and saucers. She was a tall girl, probably twenty-three or twenty-four now, and she'd been alone for the past three years since her father, a miner, had died up in one of the gold camps. He'd worked himself to death scratching a little gold from the gravelly creek beds up at Alder Gulch. He'd made a little, enough to set Laura up in the dress shop, and she was doing well, as far as Brant could see, making dresses for army wives across the river, and for the women in town who could not make their own.

'A man must take a risk,' Brant murmured, 'to make a dollar these days. The *Western Star* is a good boat. We have two cannons aboard, and the Sioux don't like cannons. If we don't stick on a bar and be frozen in for the winter, we'll make it up the river and back in a matter of weeks.'

Laura Graham nodded. She walked around the table to put the coffee can back on the shelf, and when she came back, Brant reached out and took her hand. She stopped and looked down at him, smiling a little.

Brant stood up, still holding her

hand. He said slowly, 'You're looking well, Laura.'

Laura Graham looked at him coolly, gravely, but with a small smile still playing around the corners of her mouth. 'I hadn't noticed, Brant,' she murmured.

He felt her hand in his, small, warm, firm, and he felt the pressure of her fingers and then he bent down and kissed her, It was the first time he'd ever done that, and he was surprised himself.

He felt her free hand touch his shoulder, and he put his arm around her waist, and then her hand fell away again. He lifted his head and he said softly, 'Laura.'

'All right.' Laura Graham smiled. 'Kettle's boiling.'

He released her, knowing that it was over, but not knowing why, and he watched her walk to the stove to pour the boiling water into the coffee pot. With her back to him Laura said casually, 'She was quite a beautiful girl, wasn't she, Brant, and you rather liked her on the boat. If Lieutenant Scott hadn't been killed you might have made a play for her after landing here. As it is now the situation is rather uncomfortable, especially in view of the fact that many people feel Lieutenant Scott would not have died if you'd been a little less cautious.'

Brant listened to this calm dissertation with a blank face. When she'd finished he said dumbly, 'How did you know?' Laura Graham turned and smiled at him. There was no bitterness, no rancor in her voice or her face. She said softly,

'I know you, Brant.'

Brant McRae frowned — he felt suddenly very cheap for what he'd done. Laura Graham knew him as well as he knew himself. He'd bounced from one woman, and then another had happened to come into his line of vision. He had followed the course of least resistance.

'I'm a fool, Laura,' he said moodily.

Laura Graham laughed. 'Most men are fools,' she consoled. 'You'll get over it, Brant.'

He wondered whether she meant Melodie Wade or herself, but he said no more on the subject. The coffee was good, and she had homemade cookies to go with it. Brant McRae ate, drank and relaxed. He felt good here in this little room, and the tightness he'd felt in his stomach when he came off the *Western Star* went away.

He said, 'When are you going to get married, Laura?'

Her cool gray eyes laughed at him again. 'No one has asked me,' she stated blandly.

'You've turned down a dozen men in this town,' Brant said, 'any one of whom could have made you a good husband. Fort Adams is no place for a single girl anyway.'

'I've done well,' Laura observed, 'and I like the town.'

'And when the right man comes along,' Brant said thoughtfully, 'you'll marry him. Is that it?'

Laura shrugged. 'That could be it,' she admitted.

'What kind of a man is it that you want?' Brant asked her. He sipped the hot coffee, looking at her over the rim of the cup.

'A man,' Laura said quietly, 'who will not forget the color of my eyes when he's away from me for a month.'

Brant reddened. 'I'm not that man,' he admitted, a frown on his face. He saw Laura shrug slightly. She was looking at her cup. 'Whom did you come down to see at the wharf today?' he asked her.

'The *Western Star*,' Laura laughed. 'I love river boats, Brant. Will you have more coffee?'

Brant smiled a little and nodded. He sat there watching her pour the coffee, and he found himself thinking again of Melodie Wade, wondering what she would do in Fort Adams now that she was here. She'd said little on that subject the few times he'd seen her since the massacre, and he hadn't been anxious to raise the question. It was logical to assume, however, that she'd go back to St. Louis on the Western Star after he and Flynn had made that trip up the Yellowstone.

Laura said, 'What are you thinking of, Brant?'

Brant looked at her. 'You're good at mind reading, Laura,' he murmured.

Laura Graham toyed with her cup on the table in front of her. She said evenly, 'You're wondering what she'll do now that she's in Adams and her fiance is dead.'

Brant gulped. He opened his mouth and then it closed again. Laura said softly, 'I'm not a fool, Brant.'

Brant McRae shook his head. 'Maybe,' he said slowly, trouble in his gray eyes, 'I've been the fool for a long time, Laura.'

Then he pictured Melodie Wade's face again, the perfect bow mouth, the blue eyes flecked with gold, an eastern girl with culture and poise and background, and the kind of beauty a man sees once in a lifetime. A courageous girl, too.

Brant knew definitely that he was wrong to think that he was the man for Laura Graham, or that he could easily forget Melodie Wade!

7

At eight o'clock that night Brant sat in at a card game in the back room of the Big Muddy Saloon. Rock Monihan and Walt Carmody were the other players. Entering the saloon earlier in the evening, Brant had sensed the hostility, and it had sickened him. In Fort Adams he was a branded man — the man who'd permitted army troopers to go under.

He sat there, the pasteboards in his hand, staring at them taking little interest in the game. Once he said to Carmody, 'Miss Wade staying over at the hotel?'

The mate nodded. 'A number of army officers, friends of young Scott, came over from the post this afternoon to pay their respects. I understand she's booking passage downriver after we come back from this trip up the Yellowstone.'

Rock Monihan put in idly, 'Charlie Barrett claims we'll lose our hair on this trip, Brant. What do you think of it'?

Brant only shrugged. 'Charlie's usually right,' he said after a pause.

Monihan grinned. 'So we still go,' he observed.'

'It's a contract,' Brant told him. 'I told Captain Breen I'd take his boat up the river. I'll take it.'

'You'd keep a deal you made with the devil.' Walt Comody scowled. 'I don't like it at all, Brant, not after hearing what Barrett has to say.'

Brant only smiled.

Monihan said, 'I see Captain Breen already took his boat down to Flynn's warehouse to load up. He say when he wants to cast off, Brant?'

Brant shook his head. 'Day or two.' He guessed. 'We can't afford to wait much longer than that if we want to get downriver to St. Louis. Water's falling already. If we wait too long we stay here all winter.' He looked at Walt Carmody curiously, then, and he said, 'It seems Breen unloaded the *Western Star* pretty quickly, Walt.'

Carmody shrugged. 'Couldn't have been much to it,' he said. 'Those cases of rifles for the army post would have been loaded on to the flatboat and poled across the river in a matter of hours. The remaining supplies could have been taken off the *Western Star* before dark.'

Brant didn't say anything to that. He'd been a little surprised that evening, coming out of Laura Graham's dress shop, to see the *Western Star* already backing out of its berth at the wharf, Captain Breen up in the pilothouse. Breen had turned the packet around and moved her downriver a few hundred yards to Shelby Flynn's big warehouse. He'd thought it strange that Captain Breen had not mentioned to him that the *Western Star* would be moved that afternoon, but very possibly Flynn had given the order, anxious to save every hour in making this quick trip up the Yellowstone.

Charlie Barrett came into the room, stood behind Brant's chair for a moment, looking at his cards, and then took another chair and tilted it back against the wall as he sat down.

Brant looked at him. He tossed in his hand, put a cigar in his mouth and said, 'You been over to the post, Charlie?'

The scout nodded and spat toward the spittoon.

Knowing that he would never talk without being pumped, but that he came in here with information he thought they should have, Brant said to him casually, 'What's doing with the Army, Charlie?'

Charlie Barrett spat again before answering, and then he said succinctly, 'Big doin's, Brant. Plenty big. Government's puttin' dern near three thousand troops in the field after Blue Feather.'

Brant stared at him, and even Rock Monihan and Walt Carmody put down their cards to listen.

'Three thousand troops?' Brant repeated slowly. 'Colonel Warburton doesn't have more than four hundred men in Adams now, does he?'

'Most of 'em comin' up from the south,' Barrett explained, 'from posts

140

in Kansas. It's a big pincer movement to squeeze Blue Feather. Two columns from the south hittin' at him, an' Colonel Warburton movin' out day after tomorrow with near the whole Eighth Cavalry, leavin' only a skeleton force at Adams. They figure on catchin' Blue Feather somewhere along the Rosebud or the Big Horn.'

Walt Carmody was nodding his head vigorously. 'That should do it,' he stated 'No matter how many riders Blue Feather can put in the field they can't hope to fight off three thousand veteran troopers, well-armed and probably with Gatling guns.'

Brant said to Charlie Barrett, 'What do you think of it, Charlie?'

The scout looked at the table. 'Plenty o' troopers,' he observed, 'but it's a derned big field. Blue Feather kin move fast an' the Army can't. They have supply wagons to haul. The whole three thousand ain't hittin' Blue Feather at the same time — not if he kin help it.'

'You think he'll strike at one column and then the other?' Brant asked.

Charlie nodded. 'An' that ain't all,' he added significantly. 'What's stoppin' Blue Feather from swingin' around Colonel Warburton's column an' comin' right back here to Fort Adams with less than a hundred men at the post?'

Brant felt his heart skip a beat. The prospect Charlie Barrett was painting was not a pretty one. Already, Brant could see Blue Feather's red horde driving in against the under-manned post, overrunning it like stampeding buffalo, and Blue Feather would not stop there. Across the Missouri was the unfortified town of Fort Adams with its hundreds of miners, most of them usually half-drunk, not particularly caring or thinking about the Army's fight with the hostiles, anxious only to get downriver with their gold.

There were women and children in the town of Adams. Laura Graham made her home there, and for the time Melodie Wade was staying at the local hotel, waiting for the *Western Star* to return from its trip up the Yellowstone. If Blue Feather overran the town of Fort Adams —

'You tell Colonel Warburton your opinions?' Brant asked.

Charlie Barrett nodded. 'Colonel listened,' he said, 'an' he agrees it ain't the best thing, but he has orders from the War Department. They're makin' this war back in Washington. He has to move out with most of his troop. He figures on keepin' plenty o' scouts in the field an' watchin' every move Blue Feather makes.'

Walt Carmody said, 'You going with the column from Adams, Charlie?'

The scout nodded, and Carmody smiled and added,

'Reckon Blue Feather won't swing around you now, will he, Charlie?'

Charlie Barrett shrugged. 'Still don't like it,' he growled.

Rock Monihan said thoughtfully, 'Noticed there weren't many blue coats in town tonight. This looks like one of the biggest troop movements against Indians the United States Government has ever organized.'

'It should succeed in the long run,' Brant said slowly, 'but Blue Feather might do plenty of damage before they bring him down.'

★ ★ ★

An hour later they drifted out to the crowded bar. Walt Carmody ordered the drinks, and they stood there, listening to the noise in the crowded room, Carmody said finally, 'And how do you find Laura, Brant?'

'She's well,' Brant told him. 'Figures on opening a larger shop next spring.'

He wondered as he said this whether there would be another spring for Fort Adams, or whether the thriving town would be a heap of ashes and cold chimneys by that time.

Walt Carmody said to him, 'You're a fool, Brant. That girl likes you.'

Brant looked at him, remembering suddenly how Carmody had looked at Melodie Wade, and he was wondering if Walt was trying to promote a match between himself and Laura in order that Miss Wade might have less admirers. He was immediately ashamed of himself, remembering Walt's honesty and openness in the past. Walt Carmody had only his, Brant McRae's, good at heart.

'Laura's a fine woman,' Brant murmured, 'but I wouldn't say she was crazy about me, Walt.'

'A woman can't wait too long,' Walt told him. 'Laura's not getting any younger.'

Brant didn't say anything to that because Rock Monihan on the other side of him was nudging him softly.

'Have a look at Captain Breen,' the engineer murmured. Brant looked down along the bar. He spotted Asa Breen at the far end, just tilting a glass to his lips. He downed the contents in one draught, and then he put the glass back on the wood.

'Drinkin' like a fish,' Monihan said. 'Never knew he was a heavy drinker, did you, Brant?'

Captain Breen had been drinking heavily. Brant could see it in his blood-shot eyes, and the high flush on his face. The tall, spare captain of the *Western Star* was the kind of man who could consume a large quantity of strong liquor, and still walk and talk with convincing sobriety, the only evidence of his heavy drinking showing in his eyes and the shine on his face.

Brant watched the man curiously. On board the packet, coming upriver, Breen had been a model of sobriety, having only a glass of wine with his meals.

Monihan said reflectively, 'Man drinks like that, drinks to forget, Brant. What has Captain Breen to forget?'

Brant pushed away from the bar and moved in Breen's direction. A man stepped away from the bar at Breen's left, and Brant moved into the empty space. Captain Breen turned his head to look at him, and Brant said casually, 'Mr. Flynn loading the *Western Star* for our trip?'

Asa Breen moistened his thin lips with the point of his tongue. His bloodshot eyes dilated. When he spoke there was a definite hint of bitterness in his voice. He said slowly, 'He's loading, Mr. Brant.'

Brant considered that fact, wondering at the bitterness in Captain Breen's voice. He said, 'When do you plan to cast off, Captain?'

'Noon, day after tomorrow,' Breen told him, 'and may the devil take all of us.'

Brant stared at the man, not knowing whether he should smile or take the remark seriously. Asa Breen was not smiling. He stared straight at Brant, and Brant could see the hell-fire in the captain's green eyes.

Shelby Flynn was coming toward them, having just pushed through the bat-wing doors. He looked at Brant and then at Asa Breen, a frown on his face, and then he said quietly, 'May I speak to you a moment, Captain Breen?'

Asa Breen poured himself another drink and downed it before replying, and while he was doing this Shelby Flynn looked at Brant and shook his head in disgust. Brant was watching the river captain in mute surprise, hardly able to accept the fact that a man like Breen was deliberately drinking himself under the table.

'You may speak with me a moment, Mr. Flynn,' Breen said with mock dignity.

Flynn said to Brant, 'We were planning on casting off at noon the day after tomorrow. Is that agreeable to you, Brant?'

'Sooner the better,' Brant nodded.

'Under the circumstances, then,' Flynn said significantly, 'it would seem advisable for each of us to keep in good physical condition.' He looked straight at Asa Breen as he said this, but Breen's face was set like a mask.

The captain of the *Western Star* pushed away from the bar, walking steadily toward the door, and Shelby Flynn followed him. Brant went back to Rock

Monihan and Carmody, and The Rock said to him thoughtfully, 'What do you make of it, Brant?'

Brant shrugged. 'Could be just a river man letting off a little steam now that he's ashore, but Asa Breen never impressed me as being that kind of a river man. He's had a lot to worry about on the way up here with the danger of an Indian attack almost every day the past few weeks, and with women aboard.'

'I didn't notice,' Walt Carmody said casually, 'that Breen was too worried about the Sioux. As a matter of fact he took only the usual precautions every river captain takes on this trip. He didn't seem to be too worried.'

'Reckon he's got Shelby Flynn worried,' Monihan murmured. 'Flynn has to get up to that post of his, and he knows it'll be a rough trip, A drunken captain won't help matters.' Brant considered that fact, and his sympathies were with Shelby Flynn. The army contractor had undoubtedly put up a lot of money to charter Breen's boat at this season of the year, and he had a right to better treatment by Breen. Looking at it from any angle, Brant had to admit that Asa Breen's strange drinking bout on the eve of their dangerous assignment didn't make sense, and seemed totally alien to the man's character. Undoubtedly, something tremendous had happened to make a man like Breen take to his liquor like that, and yet as far as Brant could see, nothing had happened, Unless, possibly, Breen had been badly affected by that massacre on the ridge, and was now drinking to forget the sight. It was an explanation, but Brant was not sure it was the correct one.

Outside on the saloon porch be found Charlie Barrett, a toothpick in his mouth, leaning against one of the porch uprights. Across the river they could hear the company bugler playing taps, the sound faint and now strong as the notes were picked up by the cross river breeze.

'Worried, Charlie?' Brant asked him.

The little scout spat out the toothpick, and Brant noticed that his mouth was tight around the corners. 'Thinkin' about them boys over there,' Barrett growled, 'the three hundred of 'em who are ridin' out after Blue Feather in a few days. I'm wonderin' how many will come back.'

Brant put his back against the opposite pillar and he said, 'Army usually knows what it's doing, Charlie, and even if Colonel Warburton's troop is going out alone, armed with the new Henry rifles Flynn brought up from the south, they'd give Blue Feather something to worry about. Besides, those men are veteran troopers over there, Charlie.'

'Blue Feather's bucks ain't no amateurs,' Charlie observed dryly. 'Best derned light horse cavalry in the world. Every army man admits that. Got it all over us in handlin' bosses. They kin live on air when they're fightin'. They don't need supplies; they hit here an' they hit there, an' then they're gone, an' you wonder where they went. It's their country. Brant. You ever see a wolf tryin' to catch a weasel? That's this big army movin' out after Blue Feather, big an' plenty tough, but that weasel is derned smart.'

'We'll have to hope the wolf catches him.' Brant said.

'He won't,' Charlie muttered. 'It ain't in the cards, Brant.'

8

Coming out of the barber shop at high noon the next day, Brant met Laura Graham on the walk. She'd been shopping and she. had a few bundles under her arm. Brant reached for them and walked beside her as they strolled toward the dress shop at the other end of town.

'When do you leave on that Yellowstone trip?' Laura asked him.

'Tomorrow noon,' Brant told her.

'And you'll be leaving for St. Louis immediately after you return?'

Brant nodded. 'We won't have too much time to waste after that,' he pointed out. 'It's been a dry summer and there's not too much water in the river.'

Laura said wistfully, 'I haven't been to St. Louis in two years.'

'You should make the trip,' Brant told her. 'The *Western Star* is a good boat, and I'm sure Captain Breen will reserve a cabin for you.' He added, 'There might be danger here, also, from an Indian attack when the main body of troopers leave tomorrow from Fort Adams.'

Laura Graham glanced at him. 'I wouldn't leave for that reason,' she stated. 'There are a hundred other women in this town, not to mention the wives of army officers and enlisted men across the river.'

'I didn't think you'd run,' Brant smiled, 'but the trip would do you good.' He was thinking that it would be nice having Laura aboard when they headed south.

'I'll consider it,' Laura told him.

They were moving past the hotel, and Brant saw Shelby Flynn coming out with Melodie Wade. Flynn as usual was immaculately dressed, a new dark brown coat, white shirt and string tie. There was a high polish to his expensive boots. When he saw Brant he nodded, and then touched his hat to Laura.

Brant noticed that Miss Wade glanced at Laura thoughtfully. Her face looked rather thin and worn, and he realized that she was not fully over the shock of young Scott's death. She needed someone desperately now to guide her, and Flynn had stepped into the breech. It was nice of Flynn, but Brant found himself wishing it had been Carmody — or himself.

When they'd passed on, Laura said, 'That the girl whose fiance was killed in the fight down the river?'

Brant nodded. 'She doesn't blame me,' he said briefly.

'She's an understanding woman,' Laura murmured. 'I believe she's holding up well after the shock.'

Brant walked on in silence until they reached the door of the shop. He handed her the packages, then, and he stood there for a moment, looking down at the ground.

Laura said, 'What's on your mind, Brant?'

'Nice afternoon for a drive,' Brant said rather bluntly. 'Last afternoon I'll have in this town. We might have to pull out of here the day after we return from Flynn's trading post.' Laura Graham glanced up at the sky. It was a warm and pleasant afternoon, a bright sun, the breeze coming down from the north. There was a slight smile on her tanned face as she spoke. She said, 'I can be ready at two, Brant.'

Brant touched his hat to her as he walked off, a slight frown on his face. She'd understood, and she'd smiled at him, the way a mother would at the antics of a small child. He'd seen Melodie Wade with Shelby Flynn, and he'd made a date with Laura Graham. It amounted to that and nothing more, and she'd accepted his invitation, recognizing it for what it was — a sop to his wounded pride.

He had his dinner with Walt Carmody in the hotel dining room, and while they were waiting they saw Miss Wade and Shelby Flynn come in and take a corner table.

The mate said tersely, 'Reckon he's not wasting any time, Brant, is he?'

Brant didn't say anything. He ate in silence, and then he told Carmody that he had a riding date with Laura

Graham that afternoon. Carmody's face brightened up. He said quickly, 'I'm glad for you, Brant.'

'But you don't envy me,' Brant smiled.

'I like Laura,' Walt Carmody told him, 'but not that way.' At one-thirty Brant went around the rear to the hotel livery stable to rent a buckboard. As the livery man was bringing out the horses Brant said to him, 'That trace up to the lumber camp still used?'

The hostler nodded. 'Still takin' lumber out o' the woods, mister, but reckon I'd be careful ridin' up that way.'

'Indians?' Brant asked curiously, remembering that there never had been danger from Indians on the east bank of the river.

The hostler nodded. 'Man came in here yesterday. Said he saw sign — unshod ponies — right off Sand Island, on this side o' the river.'

Brant thought about that. He'd contemplated taking Laura Graham up the trace and back that afternoon. It was a pleasant ride along the river, and he'd thought a safe one. He said, 'Aren't there friendly Indians camped in the vicinity of the fort?'

'Some Crows,' the hostler nodded, 'an' it could o' been them. Then again it could o' been Sioux.' He spat and he added, 'Wouldn't hurt to take a rifle along, mister.'

'You have one handy?' Brant asked him.

The hostler got out a new Henry rifle. 'Best gun on the frontier,' he stated proudly. 'If the Army ever gets them, mister, they'll chase the Sioux clean back into the Rocky Mountains.'

'The Army has them,' Brant assured him, 'at Fort Adams anyway.'

'Didn't know that,' the hostler said thoughtfully. 'Since when?'

'*Western Star* brought them up,' Brant told him. He put the rifle under the seat of the buckboard, and in a few minutes rode down to Laura Graham's shop.

She was waiting, and she came out through the door, smiling, wearing a brown and white dress which did justice to her tanned face. She carried a parasol,

158

and as Brant helped her up to the seat she noticed the rifle, and she said, 'Are you expecting trouble, Brant?'

'Always be ready for it,' Brant told her. 'Thought we'd ride up along the river.'

'I haven't been out of town for months,' Laura murmured. 'It'll be nice.'

'Plenty of men in this town ready to take you any time,' Brant observed.

Laura Graham only shrugged and smiled. They rode out of town, taking the trace up along the east bank of the river, heading north toward the lumber camp. Brant let the two grays move along at a slow jog, and after a while he let Laura hold the reins while be touched a match to a cigar. He said, then, 'Made up your mind about that trip south?'

'I'm still thinking about it,' Laura told him. 'If I went downriver this fall I'd have Miss Wade as company, would I not?'

Brant's teeth tightened on the cigar. 'Reckon I wouldn't know,' he said briefly.

'I'd much prefer having another woman aboard,' Laura went on calmly, 'rather than going downriver alone.'

'You could ask her,' Brant stated.

Laura didn't say anything to that. She watched the river through the frequent breaks in the line of willows and cottonwoods along the bank. The Big Muddy at this point was not much more than a hundred and fifty yards wide, and quite shallow, almost impassable for river boats. Five miles from the town they came abreast of Sand Island which was little more than a raised sand bar fifty yards long and a dozen yards wide. For Centuries the island had been the fording place over the Missouri for buffalo, first, and then for bands of passing Indians.

As they passed the island, Brant had a long, searching look at the barren brown hills to the west. Out of the defiles in those hills the wild Sioux riders had been coming for generations. The hills were empty this afternoon.

They rode on, and at four in the afternoon reached the lumber camp. An army contractor was cutting timber for Fort Adams, and there were thirty or forty men at the camp. Brant helped Laura from the buckboard, and they strolled under the trees for a half-hour, watching the saw mill in operation, enjoying the clean smell of sawdust. Brant chatted for a few minutes with the superintendent in charge, and was informed that they'd seen no Indians on this side of the river in over six months, as army details were usually patrolling the west bank, watching for marauders.

The sun had lost its heat when they returned to the buckboard, and as Brant helped her up to the seat he noticed the brightness of her eyes and the flush in her cheeks.

'Enjoying it?' he asked.

'I'm glad we came,' Laura smiled.

They watched the sun dropping toward the rolling hills to the west as they rode south along the river. Brant had almost ceased to think about Indians when he saw the riders entering the river on the west bank off Sand Island.

Instinctively, he slowed down the buckboard to watch, and Laura said slowly, 'They're Indians, aren't they?'

Brant nodded. There had been no mistake about the riders entering the river on the other side. They were brown-skinned, naked to the waist, riding small, wiry ponies. He counted seven of them as he whipped up the grays and moved sharply down the grade.

'They could be friendly Crows,' he said, 'but we won't stop to find out.'

The Indians across the river had seen them, and they'd started to yip excitedly. Brant scowled as he flicked at the grays with a whip. If the riders had been Crows, the passing of the buckboard would have elicited little attention. It meant that those brown-skinned riders splashing through waist-high water in the Missouri were Sioux raiders, a small party probably bent on stealing a few horses, or taking an occasional scalp.

The Sioux were already on the island when Brant raced the grays past the sand bar. They raced down into the water, their ponies kicking up sand as they went across the bar.

Laura Graham said calmly, 'It's good you brought that rifle along, Brant.'

The rifle and the bag of cartridges the hostler had tossed into the wagon still lay under the seat. Brant said quietly, 'Can you pick it up, Laura?'

She handed him the rifle. He could hear the Sioux coming out of the river behind them, racing their ponies into the trace, taking up the chase, and he said, 'Afraid?'

'No,' Laura Graham smiled. 'Want me to take the reins now?'

Brant handed her the reins, and then he slid off the seat, rifle in hand, and crouched behind her, protecting her with his body. The seven Sioux bucks were about two hundred yards behind, but coming up fast.

Opening the bullet pouch, Brant dumped the cartridges on the floor. There were about fifty of them, plenty to last him all the way into Fort Adams if the Sioux continued the chase.

At least two of the Sioux carried guns, and they opened fire as they drew closer. Brant picked out the lead rider, a big buck on a black and white spotted pony. When he squeezed on the trigger the pony's front legs collapsed suddenly, throwing the rider headlong into the dust. He got up, staggered, and fell again, and his companions dropped back, yelling angrily.

'Get one?' Laura called back over her shoulder. 'One,' Brant nodded. 'They're still coming.'

He took aim again, and this time he hit one of the riders, sending him tumbling from the saddle, and the Sioux had enough. They fell back, still yelling, and Brant watched them pick up the man he'd hit.

'That's all,' he said to Laura Graham. They lost sight of the Sioux as the buckboard topped a rise, the grays still running strongly, and in another half-hour came in sight of the town. Brant was back on the seat with the reins now, and as they came into the main street he said thoughtfully, 'Plenty of women would have lost their nerve going through something like that.'

'I was raised in this part of the country,' Laura reminded him. 'I'm not an eastern girl.'

'I know,' Brant murmured, and as he said it he considered the incongruity of a western man marrying an eastern girl. They were as far apart as the poles, and any man attempting to breach the gulf might bite off more than he could chew. There was the possibility, though, that a girl like Melodie Wade would be different!

9

At eleven o'clock the next morning Brant stood at the window in the pilothouse of the *Western Star* looking across the river at Fort Adams. Colonel Warburton's column was moving out, three hundred strong, a long line of men in blue column of fours, ascending into the brown hills, leaving a trailer of dust in the blue Montana sky.

Behind the mounted troopers came the supply wagons, fifteen of them, heavily loaded, three teams of mules in the traces, and behind the white-topped wagons rode the rear guard.

As the column reached the first hill, already the point riders were fanning out, and far beyond them, already lost in the vastness of this immense country, rode Charlie Barrett and the Indian scouts, watching for the hostiles.

Walt Carmody came up into the pilot-house and stood beside Brant, watching silently until the last wagon and the last blue-clad rider had disappeared, and only the dust hung in the air to remind them that a formidable body of fighting men bad passed that way.

'Good luck, boys,' Carmody said softly, 'and according to Charlie Barrett they're going to need it.'

'We'll hope,' Brant murmured, 'that Charlie's wrong this one time.'

'Blue Feather will never surprise the column with Charlie Barrett scouting for the colonel,' Walt Carmody observed, 'but if he turns and hits them with his full force before these armies from the south can close in on him — '

Walt Carmody said no more on the subject, and Brant was thinking gloomily of the other matter — the possibility of Blue Feather circumventing Colonel Warburton's column and striking at the poorly defended Fort Adams. He tried to rule out this possibility. Little Charlie Barrett understood this danger, and he'd make sure that no hostile force slipped past the blue troopers.

'We have this consolation,' Carmody pointed out. 'The boys are riding out with the best guns they've ever used on the frontier. With a Henry rifle in his hands, an army trooper is worth ten Sioux bucks.'

'Which will be about the odds,' Brant scowled. He watched Shelby Flynn coming aboard, carrying a carpetbag. Flynn glanced up at the pilothouse, nodded and went on to his cabin.

The *Western Star*'s crew was all aboard. Rock Monihan was in the engine room, and steam was hissing through the gauge cocks.

'Captain Breen come aboard?' Brant asked.

Walt Carmody looked at him. 'Stinson tells me he's in his cabin,' he said significantly.

Brant moistened his lips. 'Drunk?' he asked.

'You've seen him drinking in town,' Carmody said tersely. 'He just didn't stop, Brant.'

Brant scowled. 'Bad business,' he murmured. 'If ever a boat needed a sober captain it's now.'

'Kind of wish it was over,' Walt said grimly, or that we hadn't signed up for it in the first place.'

'Can't leave Flynn's men and supplies to rot up there on the Yellowstone,' Brant told him, 'and there's no other way to bring them relief.' He slapped Carmody on the shoulder and he said, 'We have an hour before we cast off ropes. I'll buy you a drink in town.'

'Could use one,' Walt muttered.

They went downstairs and across the planks to shore, the second mate, Stinson, watching them. The *Western Star*'s tough crew lounged around on the main deck, playing cards, sleeping. Looking at them, Brant didn't see one honest face among the group.

He noticed, also, that the hatches were down and locked, and that the *Western Star* lay quite heavy in the water, drawing almost as much as she had on the upriver trip. This was inexplicable in as much as Flynn intended to evacuate his post and pick up what trade goods he had on the Big Horn. He should have been taking only ordinary supplies for the trip.

Carmody said as they walked back to the main street, 'You say good-bye to Laura, Brant?'

Brant nodded. 'She figures she might come downriver this trip and spend the winter in St. Louis.'

'But she'll be back in the spring,' Carmody said.

'This is her country,' Brant smiled. 'She won't leave it.'

Walt Carmody hesitated, and then he said, 'You seen much of Miss Wade, Brant?'

Brant moistened his lips. 'Shelby Flynn's seen quite a lot of her,' he stated. 'I'm of the opinion she'll book passage for the downriver trip.'

Walt Carmody didn't say anything to that. Inside the OxBow Saloon they spotted the grizzled Sgt. Mike

O'Mahoney, whom both Walt and Brant knew quite well from previous stays in Fort Adams. O'Mahoney, a big, blue-eyed Irishman who'd been eighteen years in the Regular Army, waved them over with his huge ham of a hand.

Brant said, 'Army leave you home this trip, Mike?' 'Yeah,' O'Mahoney growled. 'They be needin' somebody to protect this town, boys, an' Sergeant O'Mahoney is the boy to do it. Give me good right arm, though, to be out ridin' after Blue Feather.'

'They'll need good men at the post, too', Walt smiled. 'Have a drink with us, Mike.'

'Had a day leave comin' to me,' the sergeant explained, 'an' I come over here. Couldn't bear to stay around the post an' watch them boys marchin' out. It's tough, gentlemen, when you can't go yourself.'

'There'll be other campaigns,' Brant consoled him, 'and you've taken your share of Sioux scalps, Mike.'

'That I have, lads,' the sergeant admitted.

Drinks were ordered and they stood at the bar silently for a moment, each man lost in his own thoughts, and then Sergeant O'Mahoney lifted his glass. 'To all the good boys in blue who won't be comin' back,' he said slowly, 'an' may God bless 'em.'

They drank the toast, and then Brant said, 'Army should do better with the new guns, Mike. It's about time the Government provided you boys with a weapon as good as the ones the traders have been selling to the Sioux.'

Mike O'Mahoney looked at him curiously. 'What guns?' he asked.

'Henry rifles,' Brant told him, setting his glass down on the bar.

Sergeant O'Mahoney wiped his mouth with the back of his sleeve. 'Ain't seen any Henry gun's at Fort Adams,' he stated simply.

Brant looked at Walt Carmody queerly. 'There were about fifty cases of Henry rifles in the hold of the

Western Star when we came upriver, were there not, Walt?'

'Over fifty,' the mate nodded.

'Ain't seen any Henry guns on the post,' Sergeant O'Mahoney said stubbornly. 'Derned quartermaster has 'em, I wouldn't know anything about it.'

'Weren't those guns going across the river?' Brant asked Walt Carmody.

'Shelby Flynn told me they were,' Walt stated. 'Stinson had charge of the unloading the afternoon we docked here.'

'The guns,' Brant said, 'may have been distributed this morning, Mike, just before the troopers pulled out of Fort Adams.'

Sergeant O'Mahoney shrugged. 'I came across at nine o'clock,' he told them. 'Didn't hear nothin' about new guns up until then. If they got 'em after I left that's somethin' else, but they've been derned quiet about it.'

'That's what must have happened,' Brant told him. 'Colonel Warburton wouldn't have taken his troop out and left superior rifles behind him. He may have wanted to keep the matter quiet until the column was ready to leave so that Blue Feather wouldn't know he'd be coming up against repeating rifles rather than single-shot carbines.'

'It's good news,' O'Mahoney said, 'that the boys have better guns in the field. They'll be needin' 'em this trip.'

No more was said on the subject, and Brant and Walt Carmody left at eleven-thirty, walking back to the boat. They found Shelby Flynn standing near the planks, waiting for them. He said to Walt when they came aboard, 'We're ready to cast off, Carmody.'

'Where is Captain Breen?' the mate asked him.

'Ill in his cabin,' Flynn said, shaking his head in disgust. 'He asked me to pass the word that we could leave whenever the pilot was ready.'

'What a business,' Brant said grimly, and he went up to the pilothouse.

Down below he watched the crew men cast off the ropes, and then he rang his bells to the engine room. The

Western Star backed away from its berth slowly, a small crowd of the curious gathering along the shore to watch.

In midstream, Brant turned her around, and then with the current behind them, set his course downstream. He stayed well out in the middle of the river now, instead of hugging the shorelines as he'd done on the way up, taking advantage of the strong current, and in a few minutes the packet swept around a bend in the river, and Fort Adams was left behind.

Moving downstream it was much easier handling the boat. Out in midstream, Brant didn't have to worry too much about sand bars and rocks along the shore, nor was he constantly on the watch for drifting trees and sawyers as had been the case coming upstream. Where it had taken them as much as two months to make the trip from St. Louis to Fort Adams, he had often cut the time to three weeks running with the current on the return trip.

Shelby Flynn came into the pilothouse

an hour after they'd left Fort Adams. He stood behind Brant for a few moments, smoking a cigar, and Brant had the feeling that a kind of high excitement was running through the man. He'd watched him down below on the texas, standing alone, looking downriver, the breeze ruffling his curly hair.

'We'll make good time at this rate,' Flynn murmured. 'How long do you think it'll take us to reach the Big Horn, Brant?'

Brant shrugged. 'A week,' he stated. 'It'll be a rough trip. We'll be using our spars the moment we head into the Yellowstone and start upriver.'

'Sooner the better,' Flynn nodded. He leaned out the window, looking down at the texas, the cigar jutting from his mouth. 'I put a barrel of good money into that post,' he said. 'I hate to abandon it.'

'Better to lose the post,' Brant said, 'than have your men lose their hair.'

Flynn agreed with him. He stood there for a few moments, puffing on the cigar, and then he said over his shoulder, 'What would you say, Brant, if I were to tell you that we have a passenger aboard.'

Brant looked at him. 'I'd say the man who booked passage for a trip like this is a derned fool.'

Shelby Flynn turned and smiled at him. 'The passenger,' he said, 'is not a man.'

Brant stared at him in bewilderment, and then down below he saw Melodie Wade crossing the texas toward the awning. As she passed she looked up at him and at Flynn and waved a hand. Walt Carmody had been coming up the stairs from the main deck to the texas, and he spotted Miss Wade at the same time. Brant saw him stop in the middle of the stride as if petrified.

His voice tense, Brant said, 'What is the meaning of this, Mr. Flynn?'

Shelby Flynn put his back to the open window and looked at Brant. He was still smiling, but it was not the same Flynn smile Brant had known on the way up the Missouri. For the first time Brant realized that Flynn could be a rough customer if he so chose. His pale blue eyes were narrowed, and his square chin protruded a little.

'Don't get the wrong impression, Brant,' Flynn said softly. 'I had a little talk with Miss Wade, and we decided that it would be safer aboard the *Western Star* with friends than alone in a rough town like Fort Adams filled with half drunken miners. Does that make sense to you?'

'No,' Brant snapped. 'Miss Wade had friends at the post — friends of Lieutenant Scott, who would have been glad to see her. Don't you realize this is a full scale war, Flynn, and we're sailing right into the middle of it?'

Down below on the texas Walt Carmody was talking excitedly with Miss Wade, and then staring up at the pilot-house. For one moment Brant had half a mind to ring his bells and turn back to Fort Adams.

'The Sioux aren't too anxious to attack a river boat,' Flynn said almost glibly.

'We have two cannons aboard, and they were afraid to touch us on the way up. Indians are afraid of cannons.'

'A fat lot of good two cannons will do,' Brant snapped, 'if the *Western Star* sticks on a bar thirty yards from shore and five hundred Sioux hit us. The Yellowstone is no place for a woman at any time, Flynn, let alone now.'

'You may be exaggerating the dangers,' Flynn smiled. 'I still feel that Miss Wade is safer and will be more comfortable aboard than back in town in a hellhole of a hotel waiting for us to return.'

'Why didn't you tell me this before we left?' Brant demanded.

Flynn shrugged. 'I was quite sure you'd object,' he said blandly. 'Miss Wade came aboard earlier in the day when you were ashore. It might interest you to know that Captain Breen had no objections to her going along.'

Brant looked at him. 'Captain Breen,' he said grimly. 'Is he still drunk?'

'Suppose we say he's ill,' Shelby Flynn smiled.

Brant frowned, becoming more and more annoyed with the man. He'd liked Flynn those weeks coming up the Missouri, and it was disillusioning to discover that he wasn't nearly the man Brant had taken him to be. It was clearly discernible that Flynn's real reason for taking Melodie Wade aboard was because he wanted her company.

Walt Carmody came bouncing up the stairs to the pilothouse, bursting through the door, face pale. He said to Flynn, 'That was a very foolish move, Mr. Flynn.'

Flynn looked at him thoughtfully. 'You signed aboard this boat, Mr. Carmody, as first mate, did you not?'

'I did,' Walt said flatly.

'Is it part of your duties,' Flynn snapped, 'to question the decisions made by your captain?'

'My captain,' Walt grated, 'is drunk as a goat. He wouldn't know it if the devil came aboard.'

Flynn smiled at him. 'I pointed out to Miss Wade the small dangers of this trip,' he said, 'and she made her own choice. I am responsible for her safety aboard, and I would suggest that you gentlemen do not make an issue out of it.'

He looked straight at Brant as he said this, and then, nodding, he walked out of the pilothouse. Brant and Walt Carmody watched him go down to the texas and say a few words to Melodie Wade, and then Miss Wade walked toward the stairs leading to the pilothouse. She started up.

Walt said slowly, 'I don't like this business, Brant. What do you make of it?'

'He wanted her aboard,' Brant said bitterly. 'Maybe he was afraid of competition from young army officers back at Adams.'

'There are very few of them left,' Walt growled. 'The colonel left only a skeleton force at Adams when he pulled out.'

'What other reason could he have for wanting her aboard?' Brant scowled. 'It doesn't make sense, Walt. The man's either a fool or he has something up his sleeve.'

'And he's not a fool,' Walt murmured.

Melodie Wade came in behind them and moved up till she stood behind Brant's shoulder as he gripped the wheel, guiding the *Western Star* downstream. She said slowly, 'I'm very sorry, Mr. McRae, if I've offended you by coming aboard secretly. I realize now that it was a mistake, and I should have been more open about it. I was afraid, though, that you would refuse to take me, and I just had to go.'

'Why?' Brant asked bluntly.

'I couldn't bear to remain at Fort Adams,' Miss Wade told him quietly, 'surrounded by people I scarcely knew. Here aboard I have a few friends. I believe you can appreciate that, Mr. McRae.'

Brant didn't say anything, but he could understand the girl's position a little more clearly. She was lonely, and it would be a long time before she got over the shock of her loss. She needed friends now as she might never need them again in her life. Waiting even for two weeks at a hotel in the town of Fort Adams would be sheer torture for her.

'Mr. Flynn assured me,' she said, 'that we had a fine boat and that you were the best pilot on the river. He is quite confident that it is safe.'

'But,' Walt Carmody blurted out, 'there are three or four thousand blood-thirsty Indians in the area. Flynn knows that; he knows, also, that they like nothing better than to capture a river boat with all the valuable goods on board.'

'I am willing to take the risk,' Miss Wade said.

Brant said slowly, 'I can stop for the night and make the run back to Fort Adams in the morning. We'll lose a few days on this trip, but that will not matter too much.'

'I must beg of you to let me stay aboard,' Melodie Wade said. There was a quiver in her voice now.

Brant turned to look down at her. He glanced at Walt Carmody, and then he shrugged. He kept the bow of the *Western Star* pointed downriver, and

Miss Wade touched his arm in grateful acknowledgement of his decision. She went below and entered her cabin.

Down on the main deck they saw Shelby Flynn talking with some of the crew men, and 'Walt Carmody said softly, 'The way it looks to me, Brant, Flynn is not only chartering this boat, he's taking it over.'

'Why is Asa Breen drunk?' Brant growled.

'I don't know,' Carmody told him.

'Why did Flynn bring Miss Wade aboard?' Brant said grimly.

'Don't know that, either,' Walt Carmody said. 'There's an awful lot I don't know about this trip, Brant, nor the trip up from Dakota City. Who was French Joe LaPorte to meet at Coleman's woodyard when you killed him? Why didn't the Sioux strike at our boat on the way up when they had plenty of opportunities?'

Brant just shook his head. He had one more question, a big one and a bitter one, and just thinking of it made the blood boil in his body. He said slowly, 'Why did my boat burn to the water's edge?'

Both men stood there in the pilot-house, watching the river, and then Brant looked down at Shelby Flynn now talking with the yellow-haired Stinson, second mate. The two men were standing by the bow capstan.

'I'm beginning to think,' Walt Carmody murmured, 'that Flynn might have the answer to a lot of these questions.'

Brant didn't say it, but he was beginning to think the same way.

Walt Carmody put one elbow on the window sill, and he looked at Brant thoughtfully. He said, 'What is Flynn's business, Brant?'

'Merchant,' Brant told him. 'Army contractor, and he does some trading with the Indians.'

Carmody nodded. 'And what do traders trade to Indians, not just friendly reservation Indians, but any redskin who comes along?'

Brant moistened his lips. 'Blankets, knives, axes, hardware, trinkets, any dern thing an Indian will buy.'

'Rifles?' Walt said.

Brant stared at him.

'Henry rifles,' Carmody went on, 'like the fifty cases we brought up from Dakota City on board the *Western Star*.'

'Those guns were contracted for by the Army,' Brant said. 'They were ferried across the river after the boat docked.'

'You see them go across?'

'I'm a river pilot. That's not my job.'

'My job,' Carmody growled, 'but Captain Breen had Stinson handle it. He gave me the afternoon off. Remember?'

Brant remembered.

'And Sergeant O'Mahoney had no knowledge that the Army was being equipped with new rifles. Isn't that true?'

Brant rubbed his jaw. 'Where are those rifles, then?'

'This boat,' Walt Carmody told him quietly, 'is drawing quite a lot of water, Brant. She's carrying a lot more than just the supplies we'll need to the Big Horn and back.'

Brant felt his throat getting dry. 'You think those rifles are on board the *Western Star*, and that Flynn intends to trade them to the Sioux?'

'At a time like this,' Walt countered, 'how much could a man make trading Henry rifles to Indians about to go on the warpath? On a deal like this Flynn could close up business and retire a wealthy man for life.'

'What kind of a man would trade guns to Indians in time of war?' Brant growled.

'We don't know what kind of a man Shelby Flynn is,' Carmody observed. 'You ever stop to think that maybe he doesn't even have a post on the Yellowstone, and that he's going up just to meet the Sioux — or Blue Feather?'

Brant looked across the river at the brown hills. He watched a file of buffalo move across a ridge and disappear. He remembered that Charlie Barrett had been puzzled about this post on the

Yellowstone or the Big Horn, deep in Indian country.

'We haven't proved anything,' Carmody muttered. 'All we have to go on is the fact that this boat is lying lower in the water than it should, and Asa Breen is on a drunken binge.' 'We'll have to get a look into that hold,' Brant said decisively.

'It's sealed,' Carmody reminded him, 'and if the rifles are down there and you try to break in, what do you think Flynn will do?'

Brant didn't say anything, and Walt Carmody said it for him.

'He'll knock you on the head, me and Rock Monihan, and toss the three of us into the river. Then he'll come back with some trumped-up story that the Sioux got us. His crew runs this boat, Brant, not ours.'

'A cutthroat crew,' Brant murmured. 'He didn't want Monihan, and he didn't want you.'

'He wanted you,' Walt smiled grimly, 'the only pilot on the Missouri who'd been up the Yellowstone and could take him there.'

Down below they saw Asa Breen coming from the direction of his cabin, walking woodenly toward the saloon. He was drunk.

'I'm having a look in that hold,' Brant said tersely.

'Plenty of time,' Carmody reminded him. 'Rush it and you might spoil things. We'd look like a pair of derned fools if there were no rifles down there.'

They saw Breen come out of the saloon with a bottle under his arm, and Brant watched him. He said softly, 'A drunken man is a talkative man, Walt. I believe I'll pay Captain Breen a visit tonight.'

Walt nodded approvingly. 'Reckon you're on the right track,' he said.

10

Brant wasn't prepared to find an armed guard in front of Captain Breen's cabin, but when he approached it, a crew man with a rifle in his hands stepped up, challenging him.

Stopping at arm's length, Brant looked at him. He said slowly, 'What's this? I'm McRae, the pilot.'

'Ain't nobody allowed in the captain's cabin,' the crew man said sullenly. He was a big, hulking fellow in seaman's cap, and dirty white duck trousers.

'Who gave that order?' Brant asked grimly.

'Mr. Flynn.' The crew man scowled.

'Step aside,' Brant told him.

'Nope,' the man snapped. 'I ain't takin' orders from the pilot on this boat, mister.'

Brant stepped forward suddenly, grasped the rifle and wrenched it out of the man's hands. When the crew man cursed and hit at him with his fist, Brant drove his left shoulder into the man's chest, banging him violently against the wall of the cabin. He smashed the guard twice in the face and the man let out a sharp yell.

Stepping back, Brant heard rapid footsteps approaching, and when he turned he saw Shelby Flynn coming up, silhouetted against the bright shaft of moonlight.

'What's the trouble?' Flynn asked.

'You give this man orders to keep me out of the captain's cabin?' Brant asked him tersely.

Flynn looked at the guard, who was rubbing his jaw ruefully. He said pleasantly, 'Of course the order did not apply to you' McRae. Captain Breen did not wish to be disturbed. I set the guard on his order.'

'When the captain of a boat is indisposed,' Brant told him thinly, 'it is the custom of the first mate to give such orders. Has Mr. Carmody been informed about this?'

Shelby Flynn shrugged. 'I have chartered this boat, McRae,' he stated. 'I believe I have some authority aboard.'

'You have the authority of a passenger,' Brant snapped, 'and nothing more. Please remember that in the future.'

Shelby Flynn looked at him steadily for several long moments, his face in the shadows, and then he said to the crew man, 'Go along.' He knocked on Captain Breen's door, then, and he said to Brant, 'I never liked a man who was rough with his tongue, McRae.'

Brant looked back at him, realizing that for the first time Flynn was coming out into the open, revealing his hostility. They were nearing their destination now and Shelby Flynn was quite sure of himself.

'I never liked a passenger on my boat,' Brant said tersely, 'who took upon himself the authority of an officer.'

'May I ask what your business is with the captain?' Flynn said flatly.

'I'll tell the captain,' Brant snapped. He knocked on the door sharply himself, and when Asa Breen didn't open it, grasped the handle and yanked it open.

It was dark inside. He stepped in, striking a match as he did so, and locating the wall lamp touched the match to the wick. As he was turning up the light Asa Breen stirred on his bunk. The captain of the *Western Star* rolled over, blinking into the light, and then he sat up on the edge of the bunk, staring at the two men in the room. He said thickly. 'I am, of course, honored, gentlemen, but what is the meaning of this visit in the middle of the night.'

'It is eight o'clock in the evening,' Brant informed him acidly, 'and I thought it necessary to have a few words with you, Captain Breen.' He looked back at Flynn, who was leaning against the doorsill, a cigar in his mouth, watching him quietly.

There were empty liquor bottles scattered about the room. Breen's shirt was open at the neck and he wore no tie. His green eyes were bloodshot, and Brant noticed for the first time that although the man's hair was black, he had a bald spot.

'What is the trouble?' Captain Breen asked glumly. He'd slept off some of the effects of his recent drinking bout, but his nerves were on edge now and he needed something to steady himself.

Knowing that Flynn did not intend to leave, Brant said tersely, 'I wanted to advise you, Captain, that the *Western Star* is now proceeding through dangerous Indian country, and it is quite necessary that the captain of this boat be in a position to assist in case of attack by the hostiles.'

Asa Breen stared at him for several long moments, the corners of his mouth turned down, and then quite suddenly he started to grin. Brant stared at him in amazement because he'd never even seen the man smile before.

The grin became laughter. heavy, sardonic, embittered laughter. 'Indian attack,' Captain Breen chuckled. 'Is that what you're worried about, Mr. McRae?'

Brant looked at him in astonishment, and then Shelby Flynn stepped past Brant, slashing at a half-empty glass on the table, sweeping it from the table and smashing it against the far wall. Flynn's smooth face was livid with rage, and his voice was quivering as he spoke. He said, 'You crazy, drunken fool. You'd better come out of this if you know what's good for you.'

Breen put both hands on the sides of the bunk as if he were about to rise to his feet. He stared at Flynn, his face a mottled, yellowish color. He didn't say anything, and Flynn went on savagely, 'I have an investment in this boat, Captain Breen. You will bear that in mind.'

Asa Breen just looked at him stupidly, and then Flynn turned and went out.

Brant said quietly, 'You're not worried about an Indian attack, Captain?'

Asa Breen looked around the room, at the shattered glass Flynn had smashed against the wall, and then he said dubiously, 'They haven't attacked us as yet, have they, Mr. McRae?'

It was no answer, and he knew it. Brant McRae knew it, also. Asa Breen had hinted at something a few moments ago, but Flynn had chased him back in his hole, and even in his intoxicated condition Breen would not come out again.

'I'll have the cook bring you a pot of black coffee,' Brant told him, and for the moment he almost felt sorry for the man. Breen was still sitting on the edge of the bunk, staring down at the floor, when Brant went out.

Down in the engine room, Brant found Walt Carmody and Rock Monihan. He closed the door behind him, and he said to Walt, 'I had a talk with Captain Breen just now.'

Carmody just looked at him.

'Flynn tried to stop me,' Brant went on. 'He had an armed guard posted in front of the captain's cabin. I spoke to Breen anyway, and he doesn't fear an Indian attack.'

Walt laughed harshly. 'What do you make of that, Brant?' he asked.

'He could have made a deal with the devil,' Brant muttered, 'with Blue Feather, himself.'

Rock Monihan said quietly, 'If those fifty cases of rifles are still in the hold of this boat and Blue Feather's bucks get hold of them, every rancher, every settler from here to Dakota City and north to Fort Adams will be wiped out. They'll sack towns and army posts. There won't be a boat able to navigate this river until the Army is able to bottle them up, and that will take time.'

'If Blue Feather gets the rifles,' Walt added, 'he can clean up Colonel Warburton's force which rode out of Fort Adams. He won't have to run away from them, and then after that it's only a matter of marching on the fort itself. They have less than a hundred men on duty there now.'

'And across the river is the town,' Monihan muttered, 'an unfortified town. Those Injuns will level it to the ground, Brant.'

'They still don't have the rifles,' Brant observed.

'Our first job, then,' Walt advised, 'is to make sure Flynn has the rifles in the hold. Have you noticed that he has an armed guard close by those locked hatches all the time?'

'We'll know some time tomorrow morning,' Brant told him. 'I'm scraping the *Western Star*'s bottom on a sand bar. Then I'll put in toward the shore, and you'll tell Flynn or Captain Breen that I think we've sprung a leak, and that you want to go down into the hold to have a look. If they won't let you down, we'll know.'

Walt nodded. 'It should work, Brant,' he said.

Brant went up on the deck and he sat on the texas, smoking a cigar, looking at the stars. A coyote howled off on the plains, and a nighthawk screamed in the woods along the river. He found himself thinking of Laura Graham, and it was the first time he'd thought of Laura with Miss Melodie Wade in close proximity. That could have been a sign of something.

★　★　★

In the morning Asa Breen appeared on deck, haggard but clean-shaven. Two hours later Brant saw him go into the saloon, and when he came out — thirty minutes later he weaved a little as he walked to his cabin. Breen was off on another drunk.

Moving up the Yellowstone now, Brant had his hands full with the strong, muddy current surging down at them, and the drifting trees which choked the stream. It had been two years since he'd been on the river, and although he'd made notes in his logbook at that time, the river had changed considerably in the interval. Old landmarks had been washed out; new channels had been formed by the driving current.

One spot he'd indicated in his book as Bow Bend had now become an island, the river having driven directly over the neck of the bend, forming a new channel and leaving the head of the Bend out in center river as an island. The *Western Star* went through the channel with its bow touching the cottonwood branches along the bank, coming out again into deep water after it had passed the head of the island.

At ten o'clock in the morning they hit fast on a sand bar of which Brant had no knowledge, and Walt Carmody went to work with the spars below. Brant smoked a cigar, holding the *Western Star* in place on the lee side of the bar while Carmody had the crew set the spars into the sand.

Melodie Wade came into the pilot-house to watch, and she was mildly excited as the two long poles, the size of telegraph poles, were hoisted, their bottoms set into the bottom of the river like posts, the tops inclined toward the pilot-house. Each pole was equipped with a tackle block over which manila rope was passed, one end being fastened to the gunwale and the other wound around the capstan.

Walt Carmody glanced up toward the pilothouse and signaled with his hand that they were ready. Brant rang his bells to the engine room. The big paddle wheel started to revolve slowly, and the capstan was turned. The *Western Star*'s bow was lifted, buoyed in the water by the ropes atop the two tall spars, and then with the paddle wheel driving her forward, she pushed ahead until the ropes became limp, making a kind of jump forward, settling again on the bar.

Miss Wade said, 'It's an ingenious device.'

'We call it 'grasshoppering,' Brant explained. 'We go over the sand bars in a series of short jumps until we land eventually in deeper water. No upper river boat would get very far in low water without its spars.'

Down below they were setting the spars again, and the *Western Star* made another short leap forward, and then Miss Wade said thoughtfully,

'What has happened to Captain Breen, Mr. McRae?'

Brant glanced at her. 'What does Mr. Flynn say?' he parried.

'Just that the captain has taken to drink and there is nothing he can do to stop him.'

Brant frowned, and again there was a question in his mind. Why had Flynn brought Miss Wade along on this trip if he meant to dispose of rifles to an Indian force? He could not be thinking of ridding himself of her, the way he would Walt Carmody, Rock Monihan and Brant McRae. These three Flynn could never permit to return to civilization with their story. Brant had been sure of that fact for some time now. If Flynn could be capable of such ruthlessness, it was also likely that he'd ordered the *Cairo Lady* burned, if that was the only way he could get Brant McRae to pilot the *Western Star* up the Yellowstone.

'It is very regrettable,' Melodie Wade was saying, 'that this had to happen on so important a trip.'

Brant looked down at the crew men setting the spars, sweating and cursing in the hot sun, and he was thinking that the whole business was regrettable from the beginning to the end, and that if the Henry rifles reached Blue Feather's braves it would not only be regrettable but horribly disastrous to the cavalry forces now in the field.

11

At high noon running close to a bluff Brant had designated in his logbook as Grant Bluff, the *Western Star* ran on to a sand bar, staggered over the bar, and Brant immediately rang his landing bells as they came into deep water. The packet slowed down, and he turned it in toward the west bank.

Shelby Flynn, who had been in the saloon, came out immediately and stared up at the pilothouse. Walt Carmody was already starting up the steps to the texas from the main deck. He went past Flynn without a word, and when he came into the pilothouse he said softly, 'Why are we landing, Mr. McRae, as if I didn't know.'

'I'm afraid we may have damaged the hull of the *Western Star*,' Brant stated. 'Will you be good enough to go down into the hold and make an inspection, Mr. Carmody.'

'My pleasure,' Walt grinned and he went out.

Brant watched tensely from the window as the mate went down the stairs. He moved the *Western Star* slowly in toward the shore.

On the main deck Carmody was accosted by Shelby Flynn who'd hurried up from the direction of the engine room. Walt was pointing at the hatch, and then speaking to one of the crew men, but it was evident that Flynn was objecting stiffly. Flynn moved in between Walt and the hatch, and he stood there, talking with Walt and then glancing up toward the pilothouse. It was evident that the man suspected something.

Other crew men were moving up toward the hatch, forming a semicircle around it. Flynn turned his head and spoke to one of them, and the man immediately darted off, coming back in a few moments with Captain Breen, who was struggling into his coat.

Breen had sobered considerably. He looked pale and drawn, but he had not been drinking. There was another consultation on the deck between Breen and Carmody now, with Flynn moving away to sit down on one of the capstans.

Walt kept shaking his head as if he didn't particularly agree with Breen, but finally he went aft with a few of the crew men to lower one of the boats. When he'd gone Asa Breen gave the order to break open the hatch.

Stepping back from the window after the boat was snubbed to the shore, Brant sat down on the rear seat, a grim smile on his face. Very cleverly Breen and Flynn had circumvented Walt's plan to look into the hold. Breen was now sending Walt out in the small boat to examine the hull of the *Western Star* from the outside, while he, Breen, went down into the hold for the inner inspection. It meant that Breen and Flynn did not want Carmody to go down into the hold for fear of what he would find.

In ten minutes Captain Breen him-self came up to the pilothouse. He said briefly, 'Our examination shows that no damage was done to the hull, Mr. McRae. We may proceed.'

Brant nodded. He said reflectively, 'I didn't want a slow leak in the hold to damage our staples,'

He went over to the window and he saw the crew men hoisting the small boat back to its place. Walt Carmody had just come aboard, and his face was expressionless as he went past the pilothouse below on the texas. On the main deck crew men were sealing the forehatch again with Shelby Flynn looking on.

Brant said to Captain Breen as the man was turning away,

'I spoke rather roughly last night, Captain, but I have been quite concerned since this boat left Fort Adams. We have a woman aboard, and all of us know this is dangerous territory.' Asa Breen turned to look at him. There were deep lines around the man's mouth; his eyes, though no longer bloodshot, were haggard.

'I have not been myself,' Captain Breen murmured, 'for a long time. I sincerely regret my behavior, Mr. McRae.'

'And you still do not believe the Sioux will attack this boat?' Brant asked him casually.

Asa Breen looked at the floor of the pilothouse. 'There have not been too many attacks on river boats,' he said hesitantly. 'If we are careful I believe we shall get through all right.'

Brant made no reply, and Captain Breen left. Walt Carmody came up to the pilothouse to take over the wheel for a few minutes while Brant went below to eat.

The mate said tersely as he stepped into the room, closing the door behind him, 'Now you know, Brant.'

Brant nodded.

'We can't let these rifles go through,' Carmody stated vehemently. 'What are we going to do, Brant?'

'We have a few more days to think about it,' Brant told him, 'if the meeting with Blue Feather is to take place up near the mouth of the Big Horn.'

'I wouldn't take that chance,' Walt argued. 'Flynn may have changed his plans.'

Brant frowned, and for several long moments he was sunk in thought. He said finally, regretfully, 'I could sink the *Western Star* tomorrow noon at the mouth of the Powder River. There is a rock ledge in the vicinity and I can run her onto the ledge and put a six-foot hole in the bow. She'll go down in thirty minutes.'

Walt Carmody gulped. He said weakly, 'Sink her? Sink a river boat?'

'I hate to do it,' Brant said. 'She's a beautiful boat, but I don't think we have any choice. Asa Breen got himself into this mess.' He paused and he added, 'Can you see to it that Miss Wade gets safely ashore?'

'Rock and I will make sure of that,' Walt muttered.

'I have to sink the *Western Star* in deep water,' Brant mused. 'If she lies in shallow water, Flynn may be able to fish the guns out and dry them.'

'Logical,' Walt Carmody nodded, but Brant could still see that he was deeply affected by this proposed deliberate sinking of the packet. Walt was a good river man; he did not like to lose a boat, even an enemy's boat, to the river.

In the saloon Brant ate alone, the others having eaten earlier in the morning. When he stepped outside on the deck he saw Melodie Wade standing in the shade near the pilothouse steps. She smiled and nodded to him when he came up, and he wondered if this would be the proper time to tell her about Shelby Flynn's double-dealing, and the plan to sink the *Western Star*. He decided against it, realizing that in her agitation Miss Wade might arouse Flynn's suspicions. He felt himself wishing that Laura Graham were aboard instead of Melodie Wade, but then he remembered that Miss Wade had held up remarkably well under other circumstances, and the chances were that she would continue to do so.

Melodie said when he came up, 'I suppose you feel much better, Mr. McRae, now that Captain Breen is taking over his duties?'

'Glad to see him on deck,' Brant said briefly.

As he looked at her, he found other questions popping up in his mind concerning this unbelievable plot Flynn and Captain Breen had worked out. What did Flynn intend to do with Miss Wade after he'd delivered his guns? Was it possible the man was really in love with her and would take her down river with him?

How, also, did Flynn and Breen expect to reach either Fort Adams or St. Louis without a pilot. There were no pilots at Adams, and Breen, while he could handle the packet, was not a licensed pilot with a knowledge of the upper river.

There was the possibility that Asa Breen could make it back to Fort Adams from the Yellowstone, a comparatively short trip, without running aground or tearing the bottom out of his boat on a rock, but even if he did run aground and was stranded for the entire winter, waiting for spring and high water, they were still safe from Indian attack, and they could hire another pilot next spring.

The *Western Star* was approaching another sand bar across the mouth of a little stream which ran into the Yellowstone. The bar extended far out into the river, and Walt Carmody was signaling for Brant to come up and take over when they used the spars.

Brant nodded to Miss Wade and went up the steps. When he entered the pilothouse Walt asked him quickly, 'You tell her, Brant?'

'Not yet,' Brant shook his head. 'That'll be your job some time before noon tomorrow.'

Walt nodded, and Brant was quite sure that the mate would rather enjoy playing the rescue role where Melodie Wade was concerned.

Brant said to him, 'Better get your spars ready down below, Walt.' He rang his bells for half-speed then, and they crawled up toward the bar slowly.

When Carmody went below, Brant packed his pipe while he kept the *Western Star* steady with one boot holding down a spoke of the wheel. He was lighting the pipe when Captain Breen came in behind him.

Brant nodded to the man, but didn't say anything, and Asa Breen stood beside him at the wheel, watching the crew men readying the spars. Breen said finally by way of opening the conversation, 'I suppose it gets worse upriver, Mr. McRae?'

Brant nodded. 'We'll be using the spars every few miles up above the Powder,' he said.

When the spars were set he rang his bells and they moved forward slowly, the bow of the *Western Star* buoyed up by the ropes, lifting over the sand bar. The spars were reset, and then Asa Breen said slowly, his voice tense with emotion, 'Mr. McRae, there is a matter I have to discuss with you.'

Brant looked at him. 'Go ahead,' he said briefly.

'You have been assigned to take the *Western Star* up to Mr. Flynn's post on the Big Horn. Is that not right, Mr. McRae?'

'That was the proposition,' Brant nodded, wondering what the man was getting at.

'Do you have any idea as to what is in the hold of this boat?' Asa Breen asked him. He was cold sober, his face gaunt, eyes bloodshot but steady.

'You tell me,' Brant answered.

Down below, Brant saw Shelby Flynn crossing the texas, heading for the pilot-house stairs, coming up two at a time.

Asa Breen said dully, 'It'll have to wait, Mr. McRae.'

Flynn came through the door, and he said tersely, 'May I have a word with you below,' Captain Breen?'

Asa Breen nodded. He said to Brant, 'How long do you figure it'll take to get us over this bar, Mr. McRae?'

'Half-hour,' Brant said.

He watched them as they went down the pilothouse stairs to the texas, and then moved out of his range of vision toward the after cabins. Shelby Flynn had been worried about Breen; evidently, he was more worried about him sober than when he was hopelessly drunk!

There was no doubt that Breen had intended to reveal something and that Flynn had checked him. From now on it would be very difficult for Breen to speak to anyone privately.

Brant puffed on his pipe, waited until the spars were reset, and then rang his bells for half-speed. They came out into deep water, and had no further trouble until they tied up that night on the north bank of the river.

Making his way down to the engine room, Brant poked his head through the door. He saw Rock Monihan wiping his hands on a greasy rag, and he said, 'Walt tell you?'

The engineer nodded. 'Only thing to do,' he agreed. 'Tear her apart, Brant.'

'I'll give you three bells as we're running on to the rock,' Brant stated. 'You'd better clear out of here before we hit.'

Monihan nodded. 'Carmody's having the small boat ready. He's dropping it the moment we hit. We'll hustle Miss Wade in and get ashore as quickly as possible.'

'You may have trouble with the crew,' Brant told him. 'Have a gun or two handy. We're hoping that in the excitement when we strike the rock they won't be watching you. Tell Walt to put some provisions into the boat if he can. We'll need them.'

'What about you?' Monihan wanted to know.

'I'll make it ashore,' Brant told him. 'You'll pick me up and we'll row with the current down the Yellowstone, and then try to make our way overland when we reach the Missouri. With luck we might run into Colonel Warburton's column.'

'With luck.' The Rock smiled. 'It'll take luck all around, I'm thinking.'

Brant went to the saloon for the evening meal. Flynn was his usual cool self, suave, keeping the conversation going all the time, but directing most of his remarks to Melodie Wade. Captain Breen joined them at the table for the first time, but he was very quiet, very pale. Several times Brant saw Flynn glance at him.

When the meal was over Brant deliberately steered away from Walt Carmody, and Walt, taking the hint, left for his cabin. Rock Monihan went down to the engine room to have a look at his fires.

Brant walked aft on the texas deck, pausing near the small boat which was fastened back near the paddle wheel guard. He sat on the edge of the boat, staring into the shadows along the shoreline. He could see the plank stretched from the deck of the *Western Star* to the shore, and the heavy rope fastening the boat at the bow and at the stern. The ropes disappeared in the shadows along the shore.

The night was dark, cloudy, and a breeze had come up from the south. Walt Carmody had posted two guards ashore, and Brant could see them standing near the plank. The posting of the guards was a farce, of course, but Carmody had to go through with the procedure, pretending that they were still afraid of Indian attacks.

Brant took a cigar from his pocket and put it into his mouth. He watched a man walking along the main deck toward the planks, and in the dim light recognized him as Shelby Flynn. Then he put the cigar back into his pocket because Flynn, after a quick look around, had started across the planks.

Standing up, Brant watched him from the texas as he paused — at the other end of the plank to talk to the guards, and then went on into the thick woods along the shore.

Waiting for one moment, Brant walked swiftly to a small ladder which led from the texas to the main deck. He went down the ladder, moved around a woodpile toward the stem of the boat, and then felt for the heavy rope which secured it to the shore.

The plank and the two guards were up near the bow of the boat, and it was quite dark at this end. Lowering himself over the side, Brant grasped the rope, got his legs around it, and then drew himself hand over hand toward the shore.

There was no doubt in his mind that Flynn had gone ashore to meet some-one, possibly Blue Feather himself, and if it were so it meant that they had to act immediately if they were to destroy the *Western Star* and its cargo. Tomorrow noon might be too late,

Reaching the shore, Brant waited for several moments to make sure he had not been seen, and then he moved into the woods, feeling his way carefully. The smell of the river came to him, dank, moist. This was swamp land along the water's edge, and several times as he walked cautiously forward, he stepped into water and mud.

When he reached firm ground, possi-bly twenty or thirty yards from the spot where he'd come ashore, he stopped again and listened carefully. It was impossible to tell in which direction Flynn had gone after reaching solid ground. The trees grew thick here, and very tall, and he could hear the tops of them creaking and bending in the breeze.

He thought he caught the faint aroma of cigar smoke in the vicinity which meant that Flynn had come this far at least. Deliberating for one moment, Brant decided to go upriver, assuming that Blue Feather and his force would be in that direction. He took one step and then a second, and he never saw the gun butt which crashed down across his skull, dropping him to his knees, sick, nauseated, weak.

12

On hands and knees, the blood trickling down the right side of his face from the cut on the skull, and then dripping from his chin, Brant felt someone's hands go through his coat and around his waist, feeling for a gun. He had no weapon with him because there had been no time to go for a gun after Flynn had gone ashore.

He heard Shelby Flynn's tense voice then. Flynn said, 'Get him on his feet.'

The hands went around his waist and he was hoisted up from behind, held firmly when he started to fall, and then eventually propped back against the thick trunk of a tree.

His knees were sagging, and lights were still flashing across his face. The first shock of that terrible blow across the skull was beginning to pass, and the pain came after it, a wave of pain which almost rendered him unconscious. He fought it off and managed to stay on his feet.

Then a lighted match was held in front of his face, and he looked into the cold, pale blue eyes of Shelby Flynn. Stinson, the second mate, stood next to Flynn, a gun in his hand, his small, close-set eyes hard.

'Take a good look, McRae,' Flynn said softly.

Brant didn't say anything. He leaned against the tree, waiting for his strength to return, his head throbbing, pulsating.

'You followed the wrong man.' Flynn grinned. 'It never pays to follow the wrong man, McRae.'

Brant didn't say anything. He watched the match flicker out, and he thought for a moment that he would make an attempt to escape, but there was still no strength in his legs, and Stinson had the gun jammed against him now.

Shelby Flynn said crisply, 'We'll get him back to the boat.' Both men grasped his arms then, and literally hauled him through the woods and back to the waiting guards at the plank. They left him sitting on the ground, the guards covering him with their guns, and they went aboard the *Western Star*.

Knowing what they were going to do now, Brant raised himself and opened his mouth to cry out the warning to Carmody and Monihan, but one of the crew men stepped forward and slashed him across the face with a rifle butt and he fell backward again, the whole side of his face numb. He lay there unable to move.

It was ten minutes before he was able to sit up again, and when he did so, he saw the two guards squatting a few yards away, smoking, watching him, guns in hand. Then Stinson came down the plank, stood in front of Brant, and said roughly, 'Get up, mister.'

Brant managed to climb to his feet, and he stood there, swaying. Stinson pushed him toward the planks and he understood that he was to go aboard. It meant that Rock Monihan and Walt Carmody had been taken or were dead.

He went up the planks, nearly falling off when he was halfway up, and when he stepped aboard Shelby Flynn was waiting for him with a half-dozen of the crew men. Flynn said briefly, 'Put him in with the others.'

Brant was hauled up the staircase to the texas and then down to one of the rear cabins. Four armed men stood outside the door of the cabin into which they pushed him.

Rock Monihan caught him as he tumbled into the room. Monihan had a look at his face and then he cursed softly. Walt Carmody was in the room, along with Captain Asa Breen.

Monihan got Brant over to one of the bunks and helped him on to it. They bathed his face with cold water and a towel, and Walt carefully cleaned out the scalp wound. The mate said when he'd finished, 'Best we can do, Brant. How do you feel now?'

Brant was sitting on the edge of the bunk. He looked at Asa Breen and he said quietly, 'So they took over your boat.' Captain Breen nodded. 'I should have expected it,' he said bitterly. 'I should have expected it the first day Flynn approached me with the proposition. It was inconceivable that Flynn could have another white man in on the whole affair. He intended to get rid of me and take over my boat all along.'

'They didn't have any trouble with us, either,' Walt Carmody growled. 'I was in my cabin. Flynn walked in with three armed men and they had me.'

'Jumped on me in the engine room,' Rock Monihan said grimly. 'I never had a chance. Where'd they grab you, Brant?'

Brant told them briefly of his following Shelby Flynn off the boat.

'It was a trap,' he admitted. 'Flynn saw me on the texas and be was quite sure I'd follow him. I walked right into it.'

'Reckon Miss Wade doesn't know a thing about it,' Walt Carmody told Brant. 'She went to her cabin soon after eating tonight, and there's been no noise. Her cabin's on the opposite side of the saloon.'

He'll have to figure out a lie for her, too,' Monihan remarked, 'but he'll think up something.'

Brant accepted the glass of water the engineer extended to him. He drank it, and then he said to Asa Breen, 'Where were you to meet Blue Feather?'

'Near the mouth of the Big Horn,' Captain Breen told him. 'There is, of course, no trading post on the Big Horn. Flynn used that as an excuse to get his rifles up here.'

Walt Carmody looked at him contemptuously. 'You were trading Henry rifles to the Sioux,' he accused. 'You saw that massacre of the army detail at Skull Cove on the way up here, Captain. What did you think of it?'

Asa Breen was staring at the floor. His face was still haggard, and there was a wild look in his eyes. He said slowly, almost a whisper, 'You don't know the half of it.'

Brant looked at him. 'What do you mean?' he asked.

'Shelby Flynn isn't selling these guns

226

to the Sioux,' Asa Breen murmured. 'It goes beyond that. He's *giving* Blue Feather the guns — free.'

'Free?' Walt Carmody ejaculated.

'He made a deal with Blue Feather through intermediaries like French Joe LaPorte,' Asa Breen was saying in a dull voice. 'A deal of death. LaPorte was waiting at the woodyard that night for a conference with Flynn.'

'Death to whom?' Brant asked him.

'To every soul in Fort Adams,' Captain Breen whispered, 'at the army post and across the river. Blue Feather is to wipe out Fort Adams completely in exchange for those guns, and with them he can't help but doing it.'

Brant stared at the man. 'Even without the rifles,' he said bitterly, 'if Blue Feather gets around Colonel Warburton's column, he can't help doing it.'

'There are fifteen hundred rifles in the hold,' Asa Breen went on, scarcely hearing him, talking like a man reciting a bad dream. 'Rifles and cases of cartridges to go with them, and that's not all.'

'Not all?' Walt Carmody said. 'What else?'

'Two Gatling guns,' Asa Breen whispered. 'Capable of firing three hundred shots a minute, the latest weapons on the frontier. Even Colonel Warburton didn't have any at Fort Adams.'

Brant McRae felt his heart turn to ice. 'You mean to say the Sioux will use those Gatlings against Fort Adams?'

'Also, when they cross the river,' Asa Breen muttered, 'to sack the town.'

'An Injun,' Rock Monihan put in, 'wouldn't know how to handle a Gatling gun, Captain.'

'It would take Flynn five minutes to show them how,' Asa Breen told him. 'It's merely a case of turning a crank handle and feeding the cartridges into the box.'

Brant said slowly, 'What's the deal Shelby Flynn made with Blue Feather, Captain?' He was thinking of Laura Graham in the town and several thousand screaming Sioux riders pouring into the streets.

'I was to bring the *Western Star* back down the Yellowstone after we'd delivered the guns,' Asa Breen explained, 'and proceed up the Missouri where we'd tie up below the town until — until the business was over. I believe I could navigate that far.'

'What is Flynn after?' Brant asked.

Asa Breen stared at him. He said slowly, 'You saw what the Indians did with the greenbacks after they'd stripped the bodies of the troopers in the fight at Skull Cove?'

Brant nodded. 'They don't know the value of money,' he said.

'Nor,' Asa Breen continued, 'of gold dust for that matter and there is at the present time between a million and two million dollars' worth of dust in the town of Fort Adams. Nearly two hundred gold miners have booked passage aboard the *Western Star* for the return trip, and not one of them knew that he wouldn't ever be going downriver again.'

Rock Monihan said slowly, 'The Injuns won't bother with the gold dust or loose money in town, so Flynn walks in when the fight's over and collects — maybe two million dollars without firing a shot or lifting his hand in any way. He just takes it because it's there.'

Walt Carmody said slowly, 'And you agreed to this deal, Captain, to have several hundred people slaughtered in order to line your own pockets?'

'I didn't know all the details in the beginning,' Captain Breen said miserably. 'I understood that I was to bring the rifles up to the Big Horn with you as pilot, McRae. I was to be paid well for that. Later, when it was too late to back out, Flynn told me the rest of it. We were to divide the loot in half. I — I didn't like it. Yesterday, I started to tell you about the plan, McRae. Flynn prevented me.'

Brant said softly, 'Did Flynn have my boat burned, Captain Breen?'

Asa Breen nodded. 'I learned that later, also. He had one of his cutthroat crew do the job for him.'

They sat there in silence after Breen

finished his story. Brant looked at Walt Carmody and he saw the beads of sweat on the mate's forehead.

'A whole town,' Walt was saying in a sick voice, 'and the Fort Adams garrison. They haven't got a chance, Brant, unless we can get to Colonel Warburton and have him return to the post with his troops. Even then he'd have trouble holding off the Sioux with these new rifles and the Gatlings.'

'We have to stop these guns from reaching Blue Feather,' Brant muttered.

Walt Carmody said to Captain Breen, 'What will Flynn do now, Captain? He can't move the *Western Star* without a pilot and engineer.'

'He's probably already sent a messenger up the river to Blue Feather. They'll have to come down here for the guns.'

'We might have a few days then,' Brant observed, 'although we can't be sure. We thought we had till tomorrow to sink the *Western Star.*'

'If I know Flynn,' Rock Monihan scowled, 'we won't have too much time

231

for anything. The minute he finds he can do without us we're through.'

'Then we'll have to get out of here as soon as possible,'

Walt Carmody said grimly.

'That door locked?' Monihan asked.

'Can't be locked from the outside,' Brant told him, 'but Flynn probably has a half-dozen men out front with rifles. We'd never get through the door if we rushed it.'

'Have to get out of here,' Monihan told him tersely. 'Reckon I ain't waitin' till Flynn drags me out to be shot down.'

'I don't believe he'll touch us tonight with Miss Wade aboard,' Brant observed. 'He might get her ashore in the morning on some pretense or other.'

'We'd better work fast then,' Monihan stated, 'before the 'morning comes.'

The big engineer got up and started to walk around the little cabin, examining the walls carefully. The cabin, an unoccupied one on this trip up the Yellowstone, was empty save for two bunks and a small table. An oil lamp suspended from the ceiling provided the only light. There was a tiny window, hardly big enough for a man to crawl through, and facing the side on which the armed guards were stationed.

Monihan rapped on the walls softly with his knuckles, and then he said to Captain Breen, 'This next cabin empty, Captain?'

Asa Breen nodded, and Walt Carmody said to Monihan, 'You'll never go through there with your bare hands, Rock, and we have nothing to work with.'

Brant crossed to examine the wall. It was of wood panels, fairly solid. With a hammer and a chisel a man could pry some of the panels loose, but the noise would attract the attention of the guards outside.

'We were all searched pretty carefully when they put us in here,' Walt said to Brant. 'How about you? You have anything we can use on this wall, Brant?'

Brant went through his pockets. He had his pipe and tobacco, and then in a vest pocket he came up with a small pocketknife. Stinson, the second mate, in searching him, had overlooked the little knife which had been flat against Brant's body.

Rock Monihan took the knife from his hand and opened the blade. He stepped to the wall then, and started to work on the molding at the ceiling.

'You break that blade, Rock,' Walt Carmody said to him, 'and we might be through. The safety of Fort Adams might depend upon that knife.'

Monihan nodded. He said to Brant, 'Be better if you boys kept on talkin', makin' a little noise so they won't hear me.' Brant started up a conversation with Walt Carmody. It was impossible to get Asa Breen to say anything. The captain of the *Western Star* sat on the edge of the bunk across the room, hands clasped, staring at the floor. Looking at him, Brant realized that he was overcome by the enormity of his crime. He was appalled at his part in it. There was the possibility Breen could have wrecked the whole enterprise by turning Flynn and his guns over to the army post when they arrived at Adams. The man's greed must have overcome his scruples; the picture of the tremendous wealth he would acquire if Flynn's plan were successful was overwhelming.

Rock Monihan kept working on the molding with the pocketknife, and in less than half an hour had pried it off. He was sweating profusely, and his fingers were bleeding when he carefully slid the strip of wood under the bunk.

Brant took the knife from him and was stepping to the wall when Walt Carmody called softly from the door, 'Somebody coming up.'

Quickly, Brant slid the knife under the bunk and sat down. Someone was fumbling with the doorknob, and then it opened, and Flynn came in, a gun in his hand. He motioned Walt Carmody to move over beside Asa Breen so that the four men were on the far side of the cabin away from him. One of the four guards outside came into the room and stood with him, holding a rifle on them.

Another man stood just outside the open door.

Flynn said caustically, 'I've come in here to make a deal with you, McRae. That's the reason you haven't been killed.'

Brant looked at him from the bunk, the contempt in his eyes. 'Rather make a deal with the devil,' he said.

Flynn ignored the remark. His eyes were glowing with an almost unholy light. Thus far his venture was succeeding. He had his rifles on the Yellowstone close by Blue Feather's encampment. He had only to deliver the rifles, and proceed to Fort Adams to collect.

'I don't know how far Blue Feather is from here,' Flynn was saying. 'Possibly a few more days' journey on the river. I am anxious to reach his camp at the earliest possible moment. You are the only one who can take us up the river, McRae, without wrecking the boat. I believe we can get down again. We have a man on board this boat who has handled river boats, and he's been making notes of the river on the way up.'

Brant was staring at him, unbelievingly, 'You want me to take your dirty rifles up to Blue Feather's camp?' he asked.

'That is the plan I had in mind,' Flynn told him coolly.

'You're a derned fool,' Brant retorted.

Flynn smiled at him. 'I have on board this boat,' he murmured, 'a very beautiful girl. Would you like to see her turned over to Blue Feather's bucks?'

Walt Carmody started to get up, his face livid with rage.

He started forward, unmindful of the gun in Flynn's hand, but Brant caught him by the arm.

'He wouldn't do it,' Brant muttered, but he knew that Flynn would. Flynn was no longer a rational white man; Flynn had two million dollars on his mind.

Walt Carmody couldn't find words. He stood next to Brant, face pale now, swallowing noisily.

'Take me to Blue Feather's camp,' Flynn was saying, 'and I'll put the four of you, along with Miss Wade, in the small boat. You can row down the Yellowstone and make your way to Fort Adams as best you can.'

It was a lie, and Brant knew it. Flynn could no longer permit them to go free.

'If you refuse,' Flynn finished, 'we'll eventually find Blue Feather's camp anyway. I assure you that Miss Melodie Wade's fate will not be a pleasant one.'

Brant rubbed his hands together. 'I'll do it,' he promised.

'There is,' Flynn went on, satisfied, 'the possibility that Blue Feather's camp is closer than we think. We hope to ascertain that fact very shortly. I do not trust you in the pilot house, McRae, and I am hoping that we do not have to use you.' He smiled and he added, 'I hope you are comfortable the remainder of this night.'

He went out then, closing the door behind him, and they could hear him speaking with the guards outside.

Walt Carmody said dully, 'The dirty, thieving devil!'

Brant reached for the knife under the bunk. He waited until he heard Flynn's steps going away, and then attacked the panel. He spoke softly to Walt Carmody, 'When we get into the next cabin we'll make our break from the door. There are four of them outside, and they won't be watching the door of the adjoining cabin. If we can get the rifles away from them and man that swivel gun on the deck, we'll have a chance. There won't be too many of the crew carrying arms.'

'It's a chance,' Walt mumbled.

'Some of them are on shore, also,' Brant went on. 'From the way Flynn spoke he intends to look for Blue Feather's camp immediately, possibly tonight. That means this boat will be only partly manned.'

He worked for nearly an hour on the panel, Walt Carmody eventually taking the knife from him. He'd succeeded in cutting away the hard wood around some of the screws which held the panel in place, and the screws were beginning to work loose.

Walt said grimly, 'We might make it in another hour or so, Brant, if the knife holds out.'

It was well past midnight when Walt loosened one corner of the panel. He was prying it out when the knife blade snapped. Rock Monihan stepped to the wall then, and had Walt pry out the panel as far as he could with the broken blade. Then he put his fingers into the space and he said to Brant over his shoulder, 'Make a lot of noise now.'

Brant pointed to Asa Breen on the bunk, and then both he and Walt Carmody started to berate the man for his part in the gun-running plot. They kept at him in harsh, loud voices, and then Rock Monihan started to wrench at the panel, bracing one boot against the wall as he did so.

It came loose eventually with a ripping, grating sound just at a time when Brant and Carmody were doing their best. One of the guards on the desk outside yelled angrily, 'Shut up in there, or I'll put a bullet through the door.'

They quieted down, and Rock Monihan stood with half of the panel in his hands. It had ripped in two down the center, leaving sufficient space in the wall to slip through to the adjoining cabin.

Brant went through carefully and stepped to the door, turning the knob gently to make sure that it would open. He returned then to the other cabin, and Walt Carmody said quietly, 'Ready for them, Brant?'

Brant nodded. 'Most of the crew members should be asleep now,' he stated. 'If we work fast we might have them.' He said to Captain Breen, 'The rifle locker is in your cabin is it not, Captain?'

Asa Breen nodded from the cot. He still sat in the same place, that peculiar, dazed expression on his face.

'We'll make for the cabin after we overcome the guards,' Brant stated. 'It's just aft of the pilothouse stairs. If we can capture most of the available guns we'll take the boat. Rock, you'll run for the swivel.'

'How do we overcome the guards?' Rock Monihan wanted to know.

'We'll need a diversion,' Brant said, glancing at Captain Breen. He said to the captain, 'Are you in on this, Breen?'

Asa Breen stared at him. 'What do you want me to do, McRae?' he asked.

Brant explained briefly. Carmody, Monihan and himself were to enter the second cabin and wait by the door. Captain Breen was to pound on the door, shouting that he wanted to come out, thus attracting the attention of the guards. When they were diverted this way, the three of them were to rush from the adjoining cabin, taking the guards by surprise.

'With our bare hands?' Walt Carmody asked.

In reply Brant overturned the table in the room, and worked loose the four legs, handing one to the mate, and one to the engineer. The table legs formed solid, substantial clubs, nearly three feet long.

Rock Monihan whistled his through the air and grinned. He said to Brant, 'Reckon I'm ready.'

Brant looked at Asa Breen. He said, 'Are you helping us, Captain?'

Breen stood up. He was very calm now, and he looked more like the captain of the *Western Star* Brant had known in Dakota City. He said, 'I will do everything in my power, McRae, to recapture this boat and see that the rifles do not reach the Sioux.'

'I would advise you to stay to one side of the door,' Brant told him, 'when you start to shout. Those guards might shoot into the cabin.'

Breen nodded. He went over to the door and waited while Brant, Walt Carmody and Monihan slid through the break in the wall, entering the adjoining cabin. Brant put his head back in after he'd gone through and he said, 'We're ready, Captain.' He stepped to the door of the cabin then, gripping the table leg in his hand. There was a small window looking out on the deck, curtains across the window. Stepping to the window he looked out, seeing the four men lounging nearby. One man squatted on the deck, a pipe in his mouth, rifle across his lap, facing the cabin door in which the four prisoners were kept. 'You figure he'll do it?' Walt Carmody whispered at Brant's elbow.

In the other cabin Asa Breen started to shout loudly, 'Open this door. I'm coming out. I'm the captain of this boat.'

Brant heard the cabin door jerked open suddenly, and then Asa Breen lunged out onto the darkened deck. The man who'd been squatting on the deck whirled his rifle and shot at Breen coming toward him.

Breen stumbled, and then reached out to grapple with two of the guards who were standing close by.

'Now,' Brant hissed.

Rock Monihan flung open the door, and the three of them rushed out. One of the guards had his rifle raised and was about to bring it down on Breen's head.

The man who'd been sitting down was scrambling to his feet, but Monihan's club knocked him back to the deck unconscious. Brant brought his club down across the head of the man nearest him, and he went down without a sound.

Walt Carmody went after the man with whom the wounded Breen was grappling, yanking him away from Breen with one hand and clubbing him with the other.

The fourth man tried to run, but Monihan was on top of him like a big cat, landing on his back, crashing him to the deck. He raised the club and struck twice, and the man was still.

'Get the rifles,' Brant called sharply. He snatched up one of the guns from deck as Asa Breen reeled back against the cabin wall, and then sagged to the deck.

'He's hit,' Carmody muttered. 'He rushed their guns from the door so that we could get out.'

They heard quick shouts, and then footsteps on the main staircase coming up from the main deck. As they raced toward Breen's cabin where the rifles were stored, a man came up on the texas.

Brant, who was in the lead, stopped, lifted the rifle to his shoulder, and fired just as orange flame leaped from the muzzle of the gun in the hand of the crew man.

The bullet chipped wood from the pilothouse stairs just above Brant's head, and then the crew man stumbled forward, falling to the deck. He lay still where he'd fallen, one hand stretched out toward the pistol which had slipped from his grasp.

Walt Carmody was kneeling, firing from the texas at one of the guards ashore who'd come running across the planks to the boat. His second shot dropped the man into the water.

Down below on the texas deck all was confusion. Crew men who'd been asleep there were yelling, running to hide behind woodpiles, and then as Brant, Carmody and Rock Monihan opened on them from the texas they started to go over the sides. Brant noticed that there weren't too many of them.

A few of them fired short arms, but the small guns were no match for the deadly repeating rifles on the texas deck. Brant saw one man stumble out from behind the after woodpile, clutching at his chest. Two of his companions nearby leaped over the side of the boat into the water, and then others followed their example.

Brant ran toward the staircase, snatching up the pistol the crew man had dropped after he'd hit him. He yelled to Carmody and Rock Monihan, 'Cut those ropes. Let her drift out.'

The three of them went down the steps two at a time, snatching up fire axes underneath the stairs. Brant raced for the bow, and Rock Monihan toward the stern ropes. Walt Carmody heaved and sent the heavy planks splashing into the water.

As Brant hacked at the rope with his axe he saw men in the shallow water, swimming and struggling toward the shore. He had as yet failed to see Shelby Flynn, and this fact surprised him. Just as his axe bit through the rope, he heard Rock Monihan yell, 'She's clear.'

The stern of the *Western Star* was swinging out into the river now caught by the current, and they were inching away from the shoreline, drifting downstream.

Walt Carmody yelled hoarsely, 'Boat's ours, Brant! They're almost all off.'

Rock Monihan came running toward them, axe in hand, brandishing it happily. Brant said to him, 'Get into the engine room, Rock, and have steam up as quickly as possible. I want to get this boat turned around and headed downstream.'

'Aye, sir,' The Rock mumbled and he raced away. 'Where in thunder was the crew?' Walt Carmody asked curiously. 'I don't suppose there were more than ten men aboard when we broke out of that cabin, not counting the guards ashore. And where is Flynn?'

Brant smiled grimly. 'My opinion is that Flynn took some of the men down along the shore to see if he could spot Blue Feather's camp. He wasn't too anxious to have me pilot this boat for him.'

'We were in luck,' Walt grinned happily. He looked around when he heard the light step on the deck, and then Melodie Wade came up, a shawl around her shoulders.

'Is it an Indian attack?' she asked quietly.

Brant had no time to talk to her. The *Western Star* was still drifting along the shore, scraping on a sand bar, sliding off, the strong current pulling her out toward center river. He said to Carmody, 'Have a look at Captain Breen. Miss Wade can help you with him.'

He raced up the steps to the pilothouse, tore through the door, and grasped the wheel. The *Western Star* was drifting sideways, and as Brant gripped the wheel the stern came in contact with another small sand bar, swinging the packet around so that the bow faced downriver. He grinned a little at this stroke of luck, and he had only to guide the packet out into center river now, letting the current do the rest until Rock Monihan was able to get up steam.

The Yellowstone was not the kind of river a pilot liked to run at night. There was a small cove about fifteen miles downstream and on the south bank. He was quite sure he could make this cove by remaining out in midstream, and in the cove they could wait until morning.

They were two miles below the spot where they'd tied up the previous night when Rock Monihan got his paddle wheel moving. Brant relaxed a little behind the wheel then, and he hoped Carmody would come up with the news he was waiting for.

Just north of the cove there was a small island, and Brant picked out the head of the island as they moved up on it. He swung the bow of the *Western Star* around the edge of the island, and then rang his landing bells as he moved, thankfully, into the cove.

Rock Monihan came out of the engine room after disengaging the pistons, and he moved to the bow to take a line ashore. Walt Carmody joined him, and together the two men managed to snub the packet to the shore.

Coming down from the pilothouse, Brant found Melodie Wade waiting for him. Walt Carmody and Monihan joined them a moment later, and Carmody said briefly, 'Breen's dead, Brant. He took two rifle bullets in the body when he tackled those four guards.'

Brant frowned, and Rock Monihan said quietly, 'Reckon he had to make up for a few things, Brant. He's paid for his mistakes.'

'What else?' Brant asked. 'What about Flynn?'

The mate was grinning. 'Stinson was the man you shot on the texas, Brant. Before he died he told me Flynn had gone ashore an hour earlier and was heading upstream to find Blue Feather. Reckon he figured everything was safe aboard the *Western Star*. Seems he took ten of the crew men with him to break trail.'

Brant looked at Melodie Wade. He said, 'You've heard the whole story, Miss Wade?'

The eastern girl nodded. 'It's scarcely believable,' she murmured. 'It doesn't seem possible that a man would sink so low.'

'The amount of money involved here,' Brant told her, 'could turn any minds, Miss Wade. Even a reputable river captain like Asa Breen fell for it.'

Walt Carmody said thoughtfully, 'There's the little matter of Breen's boat, the *Western Star*, Brant. He's dead and we have his boat.'

'He must have made out a will,' Brant said, 'back in Dakota City.'

'There was no will,' Carmody told him. 'Just before Breen died he turned the *Western Star* over to you. Miss Wade here is the witness. I suppose he felt some guilt concerning the destruction of your boat.'

Brant stared at the mate. To me?'
he murmured.

'You're a river captain again, Brant.'
Walt Carmody smiled. 'Congratula-
tions.'

Rock Monihan said to Brant, 'What's
the program, Captain?'

'We head for Fort Adams,' Brant told
him, 'as soon as there is sufficient light
to steer by. We'll try to make the run in
record time. If Blue Feather gets past
Colonel Warburton's column, then he
might run into some trouble at Fort
Adams with the fifteen hundred Henry
rifles in the hold of this boat.'

'And the Gatlings,' Walt Carmody
chuckled. 'Don't forget the Gatlings
Shelby Flynn was kind enough to
bring along.'

'We're not forgetting the Gatlings,'
Brant McRae said slowly, 'and we won't
let Blue Feather nor Shelby Flynn forget
them, either.'

13

The *Western Star* moved out of the cove at dawn, Brant at the wheel of his own packet again, and Rock Monihan and Walt Carmody in the engine room firing the boilers. Fortunately, they'd taken on a load of firewood the day before Flynn had captured the boat, and the wood could be expected to last several days.

Just before pulling out of the cove they'd taken time out to bury the bodies of Asa Breen and Stinson, the second mate. Brant, as captain of the boat, read the service from a Bible he'd found in Breen's cabin. They came back to the *Western Star* in a subdued mood and Brant went directly to the pilothouse.

Melodie Wade joined him as the packet slipped out into the mainstream. She said as she stood at the window, 'What will Mr. Flynn do now? He's lost his rifles, and his plan has been wrecked.'

'I expect him to persuade Blue Feather to ride against Fort Adams as quickly as possible. He knows how weak the post is at the present time with the main body of troopers in the field, and he is still after that gold.'

'Can the Indians take Adams without the new rifles?' Melodie asked.

'They shouldn't have too much trouble if they arrive there before we do,' Brant said grimly. 'Less than a hundred men can't stand off several thousand, and there will be plenty of rifles in Blue Feather's force even without Flynn's guns. Unscrupulous traders have been trading rifles to them for years.'

Melodie was silent, and then she said, 'Do you feel Blue Feather can get around Colonel Warburton's force?'

Brant stared at the river. 'Around it,' he said, 'or through it. I hope it's not through it.'

They moved downriver at a fast pace, sliding easily over the sand bars upon which they'd had to use the spars on the way upriver. They didn't need the crew men when they weren't using the spars, and down in the engine room Walt Carmody and Monihan toiled valiantly, piling on the wood, keeping the pressure up. It was hard work for two men but they worked like men possessed.

Melodie Wade went to the cook's galley and prepared lunch for them, bringing the meal up to the pilothouse, and she held the wheel for Brant, taking his instructions as he stood beside her, eating. Then she went down to the engine room with food for Monihan and Carmody.

Watching her go down the stairs to the main deck, Brant realized that she was a new woman since they'd taken this trip. She was more self-reliant, more mature than the eastern girl who'd come out to marry her soldier-sweetheart. She was a beautiful woman, too, but the more Brant looked at her the more he found himself thinking of Laura Graham, which was a very strange thing. Ordinarily, he didn't think of Laura when he was out of town. Since the ride with her up the river all this had changed, especially now that he was returning to Fort Adams with his own packet, a good fast boat, nearly the equal of the *Cairo Lady*. Once again he was a man of property, and it felt good.

At four o'clock in the afternoon they drew near the mouth of the Yellowstone, and then as they were proceeding downriver, the sun behind them, Brant heard three quick shots from the north bank of the river. He rang his bells immediately for half-speed, recognizing the shots as signals, and then he veered in toward the shore slowly, scanning the bank. He saw the solitary figure standing out on the tip of a promontory.

Walt Carmody came out of the engine room, face grimy, and looked up at the pilothouse before moving to the bow. Melodie Wade came out of the cook's galley to join him. Then Carmody turned and yelled, 'That's Charlie Barrett, Brant.' Brant had recognized the little scout standing very quietly on the shore, waiting for them, He immediately sounded his landing bells, swung around in mid-river, and came in on the other side of the promontory, the bow of the *Western Star* pointing upriver as they nosed in toward the shore.

Barrett was motioning for him to come in toward the shore where he could tie up to the trees. Brant stared at him curiously. Evidently, Barrett wanted them to make a real stopover, and not just pick him up and back off again.

Walt Carmody had noticed this, also, and he was getting his casting ropes ready. Brant moved slowly in toward the shore which was thickly wooded at this spot.

As they drew in closer he saw blue-clad troopers move out of the woods to wait for his ropes. Charlie Barrett had come back from the point and was waiting, also. Other troopers came out of the wood now, moving slowly, making no sounds, and then Brant realized there was no particular enthusiasm in this group. He saw the bandages; he saw men helping others who could not walk. Troopers were being carried on improvised stretchers. They were worn, wearied, haggard men in blue, not at all like the jaunty column which had ridden out of Fort Adams less than a week before.

It was a pitifully small group, too, less than seventy-five in number, as far as Brant could see, and about a third of them were wounded. They stood there. or they lay on the small sandy beach, watching silently as the *Western Star* came in to the bank.

Charlie Barrett waded out into the shallow water and came over the side as they were casting the ropes. Brant saw him nod to Walt Carmody, shake his head, and then come on up to the texas and the pilothouse. As he walked Brant saw him looking around curiously for the *Western Star*'s crew.

Lifting a hand to him as he came up the pilothouse steps, Brant waited, the terrible news already quite clear to him. He felt sick, thinking of the three hundred troopers who'd left Fort Adams, and he felt worse, knowing what was in store for the post and the town.

Charlie Barrett was a man who'd looked at death many times with those quiet hazel eyes, but when he came through the pilothouse door Brant McRae was aware of the fact that the scout had been terribly shaken by what he'd just been through. His cheekbone had been creased by a bullet, and it was swollen, purple and ugly, the whole side of his face out of proportion. It was in the eyes, though, that Brant saw the real horror.

'Reckon we ran into it, Brant,' Barrett murmured. 'We caught it bad.'

'Is that your whole column?' Brant asked him, glancing toward the shore,

'That's it,' Charlie Barrett nodded bitterly. 'Sixty-eight men left out o' three hundred, an' we got twenty-four wounded, some of 'em pretty bad. They caught us on the Rosebud, Brant, more dern Injuns than you ever saw in your life. Seemed like they were poppin' up out o' the ground.'

'They didn't surprise you?' Brant asked, unbelievingly.

Barrett shook his head. 'Reckon we knew they were there,' he stated, 'but what could we do? Colonel Warburton had orders to 'contain' the Sioux until the relief columns came up from the south. All we could do was wait. Them other soldiers never showed up, an' we heard another bunch o' Sioux and Cheyennes hit 'em down along the Big Horn, wrecked their supply train, an' stopped 'em from comin' on. We had to take it alone — three hundred of us against four thousand. It was a good fight, Brant, fer maybe an hour and a half. After that it wasn't somethin' you'd want to watch again.'

Brant was staring at him. 'You lost over two hundred and twenty-five men?' he gasped.

'All dead an' scalped,' Charlie Barrett nodded, 'an' the only reason this bunch got out was because the Sioux thought they'd like to celebrate a little after the big victory. Captain Wilks got us up on a ridge after Colonel Warburton went under. We holed up there fer twenty-four hours, an' then we sneaked off, headin' fer the river an' hopin' we'd meet the *Western Star*.'

'Colonel Warburton's dead?' Brant asked slowly.

'A good man,' the scout said. 'He done the best he could, but they never should o' sent him out with a small column like that. Somebody back in the War Department didn't have his brains with him when he sent that order. They don't know this is a war; they still figger we're chasin' a couple o' hundred bucks who skipped the reservation. None of 'em had any idea how big this was an' they wouldn't listen to me.'

'Where is Blue Feather now?' Brant asked him.

'We left him two days back,' Charlie Barrett explained. 'Ain't no doubt but that he'll be ridin' up to Fort Adams as soon as his bucks git their feet back on the ground.'

'Blue Feather didn't wait for Flynn's guns,' Brant said thoughtfully. 'He didn't need them against Colonel Warburton's force.'

Charlie Barrett looked at him curiously. 'What guns?' he asked, 'an' where is your crew an' Captain Breen?'

Brant told him the story briefly as the planks were thrown to shore and the wounded men brought aboard. He saw the spare Capt. Mason Wilks coming aboard, his right arm in a sling. Wilks paused to speak with Walt Carmody down below, and Brant knew he was giving the captain the story of their own ordeal up the Yellowstone.

When Brant finished, little Barrett said, 'Reckon you boys had your own private party here. So Asa Breen's dead, an' you own a boat, an' you got fifteen hundred Henry rifles aboard which belonged to that cussed Shelby Flynn, who I never liked.'

Brant went below now to help assign the wounded men to the various cabins. He noticed that Melodie

263

Wade was already moving among them, doing what she could to relieve their sufferings.

Captain Wilks came up, his face thin, drawn. He said quietly, 'Your mate told me what happened aboard this boat, McRae. We're grateful that you're able to take us aboard. Fortunately, we have a surgeon among us who will be able to treat the wounded as soon as we can place them. We've had a rough time of it.'

'The cabins will accommodate the wounded,' Brant told him. 'We have plenty of provisions aboard and I believe your men would appreciate a warm meal.'

'We're even more anxious to reach Fort Adams,' Captain Wilks told him. 'We've got to set up a defense here because Blue Feather will shortly be riding that way with his full force.'

'I understand that,' Brant nodded. 'We'll pull away from here in fifteen minutes.'

'How soon can you reach the post?' Captain Wilks wanted to know.

Brant thought for a moment. 'If we run all night,' he stated, 'and all day tomorrow, we might make it by nightfall.'

'Can you run all night?' Captain Wilks asked.

'We'll make the run,' Brant told him, and he knew what he was getting into. He'd had practically no sleep last night, and he'd have to remain at the wheel all this night and through most of the day. He was afraid to let Walt Carmody handle the packet at all at night, and even tomorrow, during the day he'd have to remain close to the wheel with a bad stretch of river all the way up to Fort Adams.

When Walt Carmody came up, Brant said to him, 'Cast off, Walt. You can have some of Captain Wilks' men take over the cook's galley and prepare all the hot food they need.'

'Aye, sir,' the mate nodded.

Captain Wilks. said, 'I understand you have aboard a large quantity of the latest Henry rifles, Mr. McRae.'

'And two Gatling guns,' Brant told him. He saw the first faint interest come in the officer's lean, tanned face.

'Gatlings,' Mason Wilks murmured. 'We've been waiting for them a long time at Adams. Very possible we might have a surprise for Blue Feather when he arrives.'

Brant walked back toward the pilot-house, passing Melodie Wade who was crouching beside the blanketed figure of an army trooper on the deck. The wounded were being carried gently into the cabins and made as comfortable as possible.

The wearied, war-sick troopers remained sprawled on the deck in attitudes of complete exhaustion, with the exception of a half-dozen who were assigned to the cook's galley.

Brant backed the *Western Star* away from the landing, turned her around, and beaded out into the wider Missouri. He knew that he was in a race now — a race with death heading toward the slimly defended Fort Adams.

14

All during the night Brant kept the *Western Star* pointed upstream to Fort Adams. Walt Carmody remained with him in the pilothouse with the mate getting snatches of sleep, and taking the wheel occasionally while Brant gulped down big cups of hot coffee to keep himself awake.

It was ticklish business moving upriver in the darkness, but fortunately this night was clear, a star-filled sky, light enough for him to pick out the occasional landmarks by which he steered.

Down below on the main deck the exhausted troopers slept like drugged men. From the cabins Brant heard occasional groans from the wounded men, and all through the night he saw Melodie Wade passing from cabin to cabin administering to them.

Walt Carmody said once as he stood at the wheel while Brant sipped his coffee,

'She's an angel of mercy this trip, Brant.'

'She'll make some man a wonderful wife,' Brant ventured, and he noticed that Walt Carmody became thoughtful.

The hours dragged on interminably, and Brant stuck to the wheel, fighting to keep his eyes open. Several times he was tempted to sound his landing bells and move in toward shore for at least a few hours' sleep, but the thought of Fort Adams with its skeleton force, and the onrushing horde of Indians now moving toward it, kept him going. Laura Graham was in the town, and that in itself was enough to keep him at his post.

He slept for an hour at dawn when there was enough light for Walt Carmody to see, and the *Western Star* was moving up an easy stretch of river, but Carmody had to awaken him again as they approached a series of small islands named the Diamonds, with sand bars all around them, and the passage a difficult one.

'Hate like hell to do this,' the mate

growled, 'but I don't want to put this boat high and dry on a bar, Brant.'

'I'm all right now,' Brant told him. The hour's sleep had helped tremendously, and about noontime after having his lunch in the pilothouse he was able to get another hour when they pulled in to the shore to take on firewood.

Down below in the engine room, Rock Monihan had plenty of help, a squad of troopers being assigned to help him fire the furnaces, and when the *Western Star* stopped to pick up driftwood the entire troop went ashore to speed the work. They'd heard of the rifles and the Gatling guns in the hold, and all were anxious now to reach Adams and strengthen the post for the anticipated attack.

Several times Captain Wilks came up to the pilothouse and stood beside Brant, watching the river as the *Western Star* churned steadily on against the current. He said to Brant once, 'I will be the senior officer at Adams with Colonel Warburton and Major Andrews dead. Captain Barlowe has been left in charge at the post, but the defense will rest with me when I arrive.'

Brant nodded, knowing what the man was going through. Upon his shoulders alone rested the responsibility for Fort Adams and the town. If he could not hold off the Sioux attack, hundreds of men, women and children would die.

'Mr. Carmody has been telling me of Shelby Flynn's plan to sack the town,' Captain Wilks stated. 'I am more worried about him than about Blue Feather now. Do you think he'll be with the Indian force, Captain McRae?'

'He was stranded upriver,' Brant nodded, 'and after he learns of Blue Feather's big victory he might think his plan will succeed even without the guns. He might string along with the Indian force, hoping that he can have the run of the town after Blue Feather destroys it. He'd then collect the tremendous amount of gold dust and currency left by the Indians, and he wouldn't have to split any of it with Captain Breen.' 'That's what I'm afraid of,'

Wilks scowled. 'Have you considered the possibility of his persuading Blue Feather to cross the Missouri and hitting at the town before he strikes at us in the fort?'

Brant turned to stare at the man, and a cold sweat broke out on his body. If he knew Flynn, Flynn would attempt to do exactly that. He might persuade Blue Feather that it was foolishness attacking a fort defended by men who were probably equipped with his cargo of Henry rifles and supported by fire from the two deadly Gatlings.

Very easily Blue Feather and his horde could cross upriver at Sand Island and come down upon the undefended town, overrunning it without any trouble. The Army, if it wanted to save the town, would have to come out into the open where the small body of men would be slaughtered as was Colonel Warburton's force.

'The more I consider it,' Captain Wilks muttered, 'the more I am convinced that Blue Feather's strategy is just that — hit at the town first, and then recross the river to lay siege to Fort Adams.'

'You wouldn't want to come out of the fort to attack,' Brant said slowly.

'Colonel Warburton left the fort,' Captain Wilks pointed out grimly, 'with a considerably larger force than I'll have. I'll be reinforced, of course, with the Gatlings, but out in the open a quick charge by the hostiles from many directions at once might take the guns. We'd be finished after that.'

Brant didn't say anything as he watched the river.

Captain Wilks went on glumly, 'I might try to persuade the townspeople to come over to the post, but I doubt if they'd do it, or if it could be accomplished in time. You know those miners. Most of them have been drunk, or partly drunk, for weeks, waiting for the *Western Star*. If we get them all into the post and Blue Feather lays siege we'd never be able to feed them, and there is the possibility no relief may come for weeks.'

It was a ticklish problem, and Brant realized it, knowing now what an army officer went through in making decisions. Captain Wilks was trying to protect two points at once with a skeleton force, and one of the strategic points was unfortified and practically undefended.

'We'll try to work something out before we reach Fort Adams,' Captain Wilks said gloomily.

When they were still thirty miles below Fort Adams, driving up against the surging current, Brant landed to put Charlie Barrett ashore with his horse. The little scout was assigned to scout Blue Feather's force and to watch its progress, When Brant backed away from the landing place he saw the scout standing there alone on the shore, lifting a hand to them in farewell.

Walt Carmody said thoughtfully, 'There's a man for you, Brant. One man and one horse out there in the wilderness with nobody knows how many blood-crazy Injuns in the vicinity. He'll learn what he has to learn, too, and he'll get through to the post with his information.'

Brant didn't doubt that Charlie Barrett would. They left the scout there with his pony and swung around a bend of the river, Rock Monihan giving them a full head of steam. At every crossing Brant tried to save time, a half-mile here, a few hundred yards there. He shaved rocks and shoals narrowly, and several times Walt Carmody, remaining with him in the pilothouse almost constantly, wiped his face with his handkerchief, holding his breath as they missed going aground by a matter of yards.

Late afternoon they saw the smoke from Fort Adams chimneys on the horizon, and it was dusk when they saw the lights, and the troopers below let out cheers.

Melodie Wade came up to the pilothouse with Brant's supper. She looked at him carefully, and she said, 'The moment this boat docks you'd better go ashore and get some sleep.'

Brant nodded and smiled faintly. He knew that he'd be unable to sleep in his cabin because the cabin was filled with wounded men. The surgeon aboard, after a consultation with Captain Wilks, had decided to set up his hospital in the town with the possibility of the army fort being abandoned. It would probably be some hours after they landed before this could be accomplished and the wounded moved.

'I'll get a room at the hotel,' he told her, 'if the Indians give us time to sleep. We won't know how close they are until Barrett gets in, but I don't believe we'll be seeing any Sioux until some time tomorrow. We've made very fast time up river.'

'Thanks to you,' Miss Wade told him, 'and to Mr. Carmody.'

'The *Western Star* is a good boat,' Brant said modestly.

Captain Wilks came into the pilot-house as they were turning in toward the shore, Brant blowing his whistle. He said quietly, 'I'd suggest, Captain, that you go ashore immediately that we dock, and catch up your sleep.'

Brant looked at him. He was beginning to feel it now, and he could scarcely stand up behind the wheel. He said slowly, 'You've made a decision, Captain Wilks, as to how you will fight off Blue Feather?'

Mason Wilks nodded, his lean face grim. 'We are abandoning Fort Adams,' he stated, 'and setting up our defenses on the east bank of the river. We'll try to fight them off as they cross Sand Island, or we'll fight them from a perimeter around the town.'

Brant nodded. 'Lot easier than trying to hold the post,' he said. 'You'll have plenty of supplies here, and you won't have to transport all these men, women and children across the river.'

'Mr. Carmody can run the *Western Star* back and forth across the river,' Captain Wilks told him, 'to pick up our men and supplies on the other side. You have been of great service to us thus far, Captain McRae, and you will be of greater service when you've rested yourself.'

Brant thanked him, and after they were tied up at the wharf, he went below. A huge crowd had come down to the wharf to hear the news. It was a silent, stunned, disbelieving crowd. As he was crossing the planks, Brant saw women crying openly. Groups of dull-eyed miners stood around, listening to the story of the massacre of Colonel Warburton's force, and Brant heard one of them say,

'Army will stop 'em. We ain't got nothin' to worry about here. I'm bookin' passage downriver on the *Western Star*.'

A tough sergeant said to him grimly, 'You drunken fool! You think the Army's lettin' you boys ride out o' here? Everybody's defendin' this town. Everybody that kin handle a gun.'

Captain Wilks had gone across the river on the flatboat to make preparations for the evacuation, and Brant could imagine the scene over there. Eighteen officers had been lost in the battle on the Rosebud, and sixteen of them had been married men with wives and children in Fort Adams. Many of the enlisted men had been married, also, and it was going to be a terrible blow to their families.

Pushing wearily through the crowd on the wharf, Brant was heading toward the hotel when he felt a hand on his arm. Glancing down, he looked into Laura Graham's quiet face. Neither of them said anything for a moment, and then Brant put his hand over hers.

'You've had a hard time of it, Brant.' Laura said. 'I can see that in your face.'

'Haven't slept in almost three days,' Brant managed to smile. 'You've heard the news?'

Laura nodded. 'It's terrible,' she murmured, 'but I'm sure the town and the fort can be defended.'

'The Army is abandoning the fort,' Brant explained. 'The defense is to be set up on this side of the river.'

Laura took his arm and led him along. 'Tell me about it in the morning,' she said. 'Where are you staying tonight, Brant?'

'Boat will be used all night to transport men and supplies,' he explained, 'and the cabins are full of wounded men. Figured I'd hole up at the hotel for a few hours.'

'You won't sleep there, either,' Laura assured him. 'This town has been a madhouse for weeks with drunken miners waiting to go downriver. I have an extra room behind the shop. You'd better take that for the night, Brant. It might not seem exactly the right thing, but this is an emergency. Have you eaten, Brant?'

'I need only sleep,' Brant said, 'about a month of it.'

They walked down the almost empty street to the shop and turned in at the door, and then Brant said quietly, 'Something I have to tell you, Laura.'

'What is that?' the girl asked. She looked at him as she turned up the lamp, and her gray eyes were calm. 'Downriver,' Brant McRae said slowly, 'I missed you, Laura. Even with Miss Wade aboard, I missed you.'

He saw the color come to her cheeks, and it was the first time he'd ever put it there. He heard her say, 'I'm glad, Brant.'

'I have my own riverboat again,' Brant went on. 'Captain Breen willed the *Western Star* to me before he died. When this fight is over, Laura, I will have a few things to say to you.'

'I'll be waiting to listen,' Laura said softly.

There was no coquetry about her, no evasion. She knew what he meant to say and she was glad to have him say it. He'd always liked this about her. Melodie Wade was a fine girl; she'd proven herself on this terrible trip up the Yellowstone, but she wasn't for him. He was a river man; he'd been raised on the frontier, and he needed a woman with similar background. He wondered now why he hadn't realized that before.

15

Brant awoke in the morning with the sun shining in his face and the sound of cooking in the kitchen. He heard light footsteps on the floor, and he smelled the bacon and eggs sizzling in the pan. It was a moment or two before he realized where he was. The room was small and comfortable with curtains on the windows and a rug on the floor. He'd slept soundly since eight o'clock the previous evening when Laura had showed him the room and then left him.

As he dressed hurriedly now, realizing that it was quite late in the morning, he heard Laura call through the door, 'Your shaving water is ready, Brant.'

He opened the door and picked up the kettle, and he called into the kitchen, 'What's the news?'

'Walt Carmody stopped in an hour ago,' Laura told him. 'Charlie Barrett came last night with the word that the

Sioux won't be getting to the river until this afternoon.'

'Fort been evacuated?' Brant asked.

'They're all over on this side,' Laura told him. 'The defense works are being set up, most of the troopers worked all night. Captain Wilks even has the miners digging up breastworks — against their will of course.'

'Walt tell you about Flynn?' Brant asked her.

'I heard the whole story,' Laura said, 'It's unbelievable.' Brant went back to the bedroom, lathered his face and shaved. When he came out he found his breakfast on the table, and a pot of hot coffee steaming on the stove, and he had a visitor.

Little Charlie Barrett, his face still haggard and swollen, sat in the chair opposite him, finishing his second cup of coffee. He said simply, 'Carmody said you were down here, Brant.'

'How does it look?' Brant asked him.

'Bad,' the scout sighed. 'Reckon I don't like it, Brant.'

Brant stared at him. 'But the Army had to abandon the post, Charlie. Blue Feather would have crossed the river and hit here first.'

'Know that,' Charlie nodded, 'but there ain't no way this town kin be defended, Brant. Ain't enough soldiers to go around to begin with. Them derned miners. ain't doin' much fightin'. Blue Feather will find a weak spot an' come right through, an' once they're in town it'll be over.'

Brant looked at the platter of bacon and eggs in front of him. Then he looked at Laura Graham who was pouring his coffee. Her hand was very steady, and she did not spill a drop. She'd heard Charlie's remarks.

'You tell Captain Wilks your opinion?' Brant asked.

The scout shrugged. 'Can't tell the Army nothin',' he said stubbornly. 'Told 'em they never should o' left the post to begin with.'

Brant gulped down the breakfast, washed it down with two cups of coffee, and then left with Charlie Barrett to find Captain Wilks. They spotted the officer at work near one of the rude breast-works which had been thrown across the road leading north toward Sand Island. The lean captain was having a time of it with half a hundred miners who were carrying out his instructions only halfheartedly.

'How do you feel, Captain McRae?' Wilks asked solicitously when Brant came up.

Brant wasted no time. 'Charlie thinks these defenses will not hold against Blue Feather's attack,' he said grimly. 'I'd take Charlie's warning if I were you, Captain.'

Captain Wilks' lips tightened. 'I've always had the highest respect for Charlie Barrett,' he said stiffly, 'but what can we do?'

Barrett said, 'You ain't stoppin' 'em at Sand Island, either, Captain. Ain't more than a foot o' water at the fordin' place, an' they'll keep comin'. You can't set up defenses along there because there ain't any trees or rocks. It's flat land. They'll shoot the hell out o' you.'

Captain Wilks shook his head. 'Then the defense of the town will have to be made here on the outskirts of town.'

Charlie looked at the breastworks dubiously, and then he glanced at Brant who was looking down along the river. From this point Brant could see the pilothouse of the *Western Star* above the rooftops.

Across the river the red tide was moving toward them at this very moment. It was only a matter of a few hours before they reached the Missouri.

Captain Wilks said to Brant, 'Do you have any suggestions, Captain McRae?'

Brant looked at him. 'We can't set up the defense at Sand Island, and we can't defend this town at every point. There's only one other place we can fight.'

Where is that?' Captain Wilks asked curiously.

'From the deck of the *Western Star*,' Brant told him quietly. 'We'll have a moving fortress in between the abandoned fort and the town of Fort Adams. The Sioux will have to knock us out to get across the river, and they might have a time doing that because we won't be standing still. We can move from one place to the other. With a hundred troopers on board with Henry rifles, Captain, and plenty of ammunition, and with the two Gatlings mounted in the bow and in the stern—'

Charlie Barrett was grinning broadly, 'Regular gunboat,' he chuckled. 'We'll blast them Injuns.'

'Can you navigate to Sand Island?' Captain Willes wanted to know.

Brant nodded. 'We can get up to the island,' he stated, 'and prevent the Indians from crossing there. If the men shoot from behind fortifications on the deck, and we manage to keep the Gatlings going, they won't cross.'

Captain Wilks said to Charlie Barrett, 'How many hours do you think we have, Charlie?'

Charlie shrugged. 'Take 'em a little time to burn the post across the river,' he stated. 'I'd say four hours before they start to come across up at the island.'

The army officer looked at Brant. 'That enough?' he asked.

'Plenty,' Brant told him.

Captain Wilks made the arrangements to return the Gatlings to the deck of the *Western Star* and set up his fortifications. Brant went immediately to the packet and found Walt Carmody waiting for him. Walt looked peaked, also, from his work the previous night ferrying the troops across the river.

He watched the troopers hurrying aboard, and he said to Brant, curiously, 'What's happening, Brant?'

'We're making a gunboat out of the *Western Star*,' Brant told him briefly, 'and then we're running up to Sand Island to prevent the Sioux from crossing.'

Walt Carmody's black eyes glistened. 'Good,' he murmured. 'Very good, Brant.'

'How is Miss Wade?' Brant asked him.

'Still with the men in the cabins,' Walt explained. 'She worked all through the night. Wounded men call her an angel of mercy.'

Brant nodded and smiled. 'A fine girl, Walt. Like I told you, she'll make somebody a good wife.'

Walt Carmody just nodded, and Brant said, 'When this is over, Walt, I'm asking somebody to marry me.'

'That so,' Walt muttered. His jaw started to sag a little.

'Laura Graham,' Brant told him. He went up to the engine room, leaving Walt staring after him, the happiness coming into his eyes. Rock Monihan was tinkering with the engine, and Brant ordered him to get up steam immediately.

'We pullin' out?' The Rock asked incredulously.

'The *Western Star* is moving into the fight,' Brant told him. 'She's being fortified like the Rock of Gibraltar.'

'Glory be,' Rock Monihan exclaimed when Brant had explained the plan to him.

Troopers were swarming on to the Western Star when Brant came out of the engine room. Under the direction of noncommissioned officers they were erecting barricades on the portside of the texas and main decks, rolling boxes and barrels up from the hold, hauling on board sandbags.

The two Gatlings which had been taken off were rolled back across the planks and set up on the main deck in the bow and the stern. Captain Wilks came over to where Brant was directing some of the work, and he said, 'Going along smoothly, Captain McRae. I have a hundred men aboard equipped with three Henry rifles apiece, and plenty of ammunition to keep them shooting all through the night. There is a skeleton force ashore in case any of the hostiles do cross the river and descend upon the town.'

'They'll be handicapped coming into the water at the island,' Brant stated, 'and they won't be coming fast. When those Gatlings open up on them, it'll go pretty hard.' He watched the troopers handling the Gatlings, grinning, laughing, examining the new guns with much interest, and then covering them with tarpaulins which would be thrown off when the fight began.

'My only big concern now,' Wilks said, 'is that we'll stick on a bar up near Sand Island and be unable to manoeuvre.'

'We won't stick,' Brant promised him.

'Then we'll make them sweat,' Captain Wilks promised grimly. 'They'll pay for that slaughter of our troops on the Rosebud River.'

'I'd suggest,' Brant said, 'that we move the *Western Star* up to the island now, and tie up a few hundred yards below. They won't know what we intend to do, and when they come out into the river we'll steam in between the island and the east bank, and have them out in midstream.'

'Very good,' Wilks nodded.

Brant went up to the pilothouse while Walt Carmody had the ropes cast off below. He rang his bells to the engine room, and Rock Monihan put the pistons in gear, backing the *Western Star* away from its berth.

They were moving leisurely upriver, a big crowd on the shore watching silently. It was three o'clock in the afternoon, and there was the cloud of dust rolling in from the west.

Charlie Barrett sitting in the pilot-house spat out the window and said, 'Right on time, Brant.'

'How many do you figure?' Brant asked him.

'More dern Injuns than any of us have seen together in one place,' Barrett told him, 'an' all of 'em hopped up 'cause they won a big victory.'

'I don't like it,' Brant murmured, 'that Shelby Flynn is with that bunch. He knows what we have aboard this boat, and he might try to persuade Blue Feather to go far upriver to make the crossing.'

Charlie Barrett shook his head. 'Ain't a fordin' place fer horses within fifty miles o' Sand Island,' he stated, 'an them Injuns think their medicine is good. They figure nothin' kin stop 'em.'

Brant looked down at the troopers on deck. They were rested now after their bitter fight on the Rosebud, and they were confident despite the huge odds. They sat behind their sandbag barricade talking in low tones, watching that dust cloud in the west.

Melodie Wade had gone ashore with the wounded men when they'd been transferred. Brant had had a brief glimpse of her striding down the gangplank beside a stretcher case. She'd waved a cheery hand to him up in the pilothouse and then had gone on to the improvised hospital ashore.

Captain Wilks came into the pilothouse with Walt Carmody as they were pulling in toward the shore just below the island. Brant spoke to Monihan through the speaking tube, telling him to keep his steam up every moment from now on, and wait for the bells.

'Aye, sir,' The Rock acknowledged.

Captain Wilks said to Charlie Barrett,

'Do you think they'll try to make the crossing this afternoon, Charlie?'

Little Barrett shrugged. 'Burnin' the fort will keep 'em happy and occupied for a while,' he observed. 'Reckon they'll wait till the mornin' before they come over fer their fight.'

'How about tonight?' Captain Wilks wanted to know.

'Injuns don't fight at night,' Charlie Barrett stated.

Something clicked in Brant McRae's mind. Since reaching Sand Island he'd been conscious of the fact that a big doubt gnawed at his mind. It was too easy — much too easy. He said thoughtfully, 'Wouldn't they make an exception, Charlie?'

'Ain't never met an Injun who would fight after dark,' Charlie Barett said with conviction. 'Afraid o' evil spirits.'

'What if a man like Shelby Flynn were pushing them?' Brant went on. 'Suppose he were able to convince Blue Feather that it would be suicide trying to make the crossing in the daytime, but that they'd have a good chance of getting over under cover of night.'

Charlie Barrett shook his head dubiously. 'Ain't no tellin' what an Injun will do, Brant. I'm only sayin' what they've done in the past. It could be that they'd think Blue Feather's medicine was good after he licked Colonel Warburton's force on the Rosebud. They might go along with him if Flynn persuaded Blue Feather to go it at night.'

Captain Wilks' thin face showed his worry as he watched that ominous cloud of dust beyond the hills. Already, the first few streamers of riders had come down through defiles in the hills, and they were fanning out as they approached the silent army post.

The flatboat carrying the last load taken from Fort Adams pushed away from the shore and crossed to the east bank.

The crowd at the wharf was silent, a bitter crowd and an apprehensive crowd.

Captain Wilks said slowly, 'Do you think they'll try to make the crossing tonight, Captain McRae?'

'I know Shelby Flynn,' Brant told him, 'and he knows what we have on board the *Western Star*. The Sioux have never seen Gatling guns in action, but Flynn probably has. He'll know that they haven't a chance of getting over in broad daylight, but a good chance of making it at night. At this very moment he'll be arguing with Blue Feather, trying to convince him that he has to wait for the darkness.'

'We'll have to prepare for such an eventuality, Captain,' Wilks muttered.

'How about building brush fires on the sand bar,' Walt Carmody put in.

Brant shook his head. 'They'd just wait until the fires burned down,' he stated, 'and we'd be unable to keep them up because the Sioux could fire on us from the other shore.'

'Do you have any suggestions?' Captain Wilks asked.

They were watching the Indian bands move nearer and nearer to the abandoned post, riding in, yelling. firing, attempting to draw return fire.

Brant said thoughtfully, 'If we could dig up a half-dozen wire baskets in town we might be able to fix something up.'

'How's that?' Captain Wilks asked curiously.

'We could fasten a few long green poles out over the side of the *Western Star*,' Brant told him. 'Hook the wire baskets to the poles, and then fill the baskets with oiled rags. When the Sioux start their drive we light the oiled rags and move into the channel.'

Captain Wilks snapped his fingers. 'It should work, Captain,' he smiled, and immediately he sent a few men ashore to locate wire baskets in town. Another detail went ashore to cut the green poles which would hold the baskets.

On the texas deck they continued to watch the antics of the Sioux as they moved closer and closer to the walls of the fort. The main body of the Indians was coming up now, covering the hillsides. Ascertaining that the post had been abandoned, they entered, whooping wildly. In a very few minutes billows of smoke started to lift up into the blue afternoon sky as building after building was ignited, Walt Carmody said to Brant, 'There she goes, an' I'm glad nobody's in it.'

Small bands of Indians roamed up and down along the west bank of the river, some of them riding as far north as Sand Island, but the crossing was not made.

The *Western Star* was poised on the east bank, with crew men ready to cast off ropes at a moment's notice. Brant stood in the pilothouse now, watching the scene on the other shore. Steam hissed through the gauge cocks, and they were ready to move.

Walt Carmody and Charlie Barrett stood in the pilothouse, watching, saying little as Fort Adams literally exploded into flame. A huge pall of smoke hung over the river now, and occasionally bunches of Sioux rode their ponies down into the water, yelling, brandishing their guns savagely.

At four in the afternoon the shore detail returned with four fifteen-foot poles, green lodgepoles the Sioux used in their tepees. A half-dozen wire baskets had been located in the town, and they also were aboard.

Brant watched Walt Carmody direct the crew men as they fastened the poles to the main deck, and readied the wire baskets. Oiled rags were brought up from the engine room, piled into the baskets, and the baskets rigged to the ends of the poles.

Charlie Barrett said to Brant as they watched the proceedings, and as the sun went down behind the hills, 'Reckon you're right, Brant. They ain't attackin' today. Wouldn't be surprised now if Blue Feather got 'em to come across to night.'

Walt Carmody came up to say that the fire baskets were ready, and the three men stood in the pilothouse watching the red flames lick along the wooden palisade of Fort Adams. Carmody said, 'Captain Wilks has four troopers on Sand Island. At the first sign of movement out from the shore they will fire three quick shots before they head for the shore. That'll be the signal for us to head for the channel.'

Brant nodded. 'We can still hope,' he said, 'that they don't come across till dawn, when we can see them.'

The night shadows fell across the river which was illuminated halfway across by the flames from the burning Fort Adams. The fierce yelling on the other bank had gradually subsided. The night was clear with no moon again, but plenty of starlight.

A crew man came up to the pilothouse with coffee and a platter of hot meat and potatoes. Brant ate from the rear seat of the pilothouse, which was illuminated with a single small lantern. An ominous silence spread over the Missouri. On the east bank the townspeople waited, the men behind the breastworks, the women in the town, waiting and listening.

No sounds came from the west bank as the flames gradually died down. Brant watched building after building collapse in fiery ruins, sending huge showers of sparks into the night sky. The Sioux force either had withdrawn to the hills, or were waiting on the darkened shore in silence.

There were no campfires, and this in itself was a sign that something was about to happen. Walt Carmody drank his coffee with Brant, and then both men smoked cigars as the long minutes passed by. On the deck the troopers waited behind their barricades, having been informed that the Indians might attempt a night crossing.

'If they're not eating over there,' Carmody muttered, 'it might mean that they figure on being in the town tonight. A force as big as that would have hundreds of campfires going now if they intended to remain over till morning. Even if they were back in the hills we'd see the glow of the fires.'

'But there are no fires,' Brant said.

'Then they'll attack,' Carmody said grimly.

'I think so,' Brant nodded. He reached out for his coffee cup to finish the remaining half cup, and then he heard three quick shots from the direction of Sand Island.

'That's it,' Walt Carmody said. There was no emotion in his voice. It was a simple statement of fact as if one man were telling another that the dinner bell had rung.

16

The ropes were cast from the *Western Star* just as several thousand screaming, naked, painted Indians tore down a sand bluff into the shallow water, splashing out toward the sand bar in mid-river. The sound was deafening. Walt Carmody disappeared through the pilothouse door, and Brant pointed the bow of the packet toward the channel between the island and the east shore. Down below on the deck, crew men were igniting the oiled rags in the wire baskets, swinging them out to the end of the poles along the port side of the boat.

In the flickering light of the burning rags Brant could see the line of bluejacketed troopers crouching behind the breastworks on the main deck and on the texas, and he saw, too, the squat, metallic barrels of the Gatlings, the tarpaulins stripped from them, ready for action, one man at the crank, another ready to feed the cartridges into the box, and a third standing by with fresh cartridges.

Capt. Mason Wilks stood near the bow Gatling, staring toward the island. They could see nothing, but the sound of those thousands of horsemen coming into the river, splashing, screeching, was indescribable.

The *Western Star* moved toward the passage silently in contrast, and the bow of the packet came up to the southern tip of the sand bar just as the first scattered groups of Indians scrambled out of the water, their ponies' hoofs churning up the sand as they tried to drive across the bar.

There were probably a hundred of them on the bar when the bow Gatling went into action. Flame spat from the chunky barrel of the gun, and a stream of bullets tore into the swiftly moving Indian riders on the bar.

Ponies and riders went down, threshing in the sand, the ponies screaming as the bullets tore into them. It was as if a huge scythe had been swept across the bar, cutting down every object in its way.

Then the *Western Star* slid gently in to the channel, Brant at the wheel, crouching a little because several bullets had already come through the pilothouse window. He steered carefully, remembering exactly where the *Western Star* had touched in the afternoon on the practice run.

The light from the burning rags illuminated the entire bar as hundreds upon hundreds of the Sioux clambered up out of the water and raced their ponies directly toward the slowly-moving packet.

The *Western Star* was within twenty yards of the sand bar, and Indians were crashing down into the water from the bar, hoping to clamber aboard, when the riflemen opened up on the main and texas decks.

Sheets of flame burst from the Henry guns, and long lines of the hostiles were torn to pieces. Riders fell into the water and were swept downriver in the current.

Riderless horses turned back from the burning baskets, screaming with fright, turned upon other hundreds who were driving across the sand bar, creating a horrible turmoil.

Into this mass of riders almost hopelessly entangled, both Gatling guns opened fire, levelling them to the ground. The riflemen fired into the mob still coming on to the island, driven by those behind them.

Indian riders went down into the shallow water and were trampled by others coming up, and still the Henry rifles cracked, an almost continuous roar, and the Gatlings sang their song of death.

A small, determined band of the Sioux swept across the northern tip of the bar and came straight toward the *Western Star*. The nearest riders were within a few yards of the boat, in under the overhanging baskets, when they were shot down.

Brant had already rung his bells, and the packet had stopped in the channel, the paddle wheel revolving slowly, holding the boat against the current. The troopers continued to fire from the decks, picking up one rifle after the other, emptying them, and then reloading as fast as they could.

The back of the Sioux attack was broken. Their return fire was trifling in comparison with the heavy volume of fire from the packet. Lead caromed off the steel-reinforced pilothouse walls as Indian riflemen tried to kill the pilot, but Brant, crouching low, was protected.

In the middle of the fight he'd had a glimpse of a big Indian in full war bonnet, riding a pure white horse, leading a charge across the bar. The charge had ended with one long burst from the bow Gatling, and the Indian with the war bonnet had been literally blown apart by the stream of bullets. He'd fallen into six inches of water at the edge of the sand bar, and he lay there now, the feathers of his bonnet floating in the water, his face down.

Down below on the texas Brant saw Charlie Barrett pointing excitedly toward this Indian, shouting to Captain Wilks, and Brant surmised that the Indian on the white pony had been Blue Feather, himself.

There were no more Sioux coming up on to the sand bar. Brant could still hear them in the water on the opposite side of the bar, but they were returning to the west bank of the Missouri, a riddled, terrified mob, fleeing back to their villages, their power broken.

Walt Carmody broke into the pilothouse, yelling, pounding Brant's back.

'It's over,' Carmody whooped. 'It's all over, Brant.'

Brant stared at the wreckage as he rang his bells and the *Western Star* backed out of the channel again. Almost every square foot of the little bar was covered with dead Indians and horses. Wounded men were trying feebly to crawl back into the water and make their way to the west bank. Others lay in the water, partly submerged, with the current moving them slowly.

In the flickering light of the burning oil rags, Brant saw one buck, wounded to the death, sitting up on the sand, blood streaming from chest wounds, as he tried with feeble fingers to set an arrow into his bow. He scarcely had the strength to bend the bow, and when he got the arrow off it fell into the water before reaching the packet. He fell backward after discharging the arrow.

Watching him, Brant had the feeling that it was symbolic of the red man's desperate, brave and yet futile fight against the white invaders. On the wings of what had been their greatest victory they had been reduced, to nothing.

'That buck on the white horse, the one with the war bonnet,' Walt Carmody was saying excitedly, 'was Blue Feather. The Sioux are finished, Brant.'

Brant nodded. 'You see Flynn in the fight?' he asked.

'He'd be waiting on the other shore,' Carmody said contemptuously. 'He wouldn't run against those Gatlings or his own Henry rifles.'

'What'll he do now?' Brant murmured.

'It's a big country,' Walt Carmody shrugged. 'Reckon he can go anywhere and start over again, Brant.'

Brant didn't say anything to that. He turned the *Western Star* around in the river and headed back to the town. The news had already reached them that the Sioux attack had been repelled, and that the Sioux were now fleeing back into the hills.

Almost the entire town had assembled at the wharf as the *Western Star* moved slowly in toward its berth. Brant listened to the noise, the cheering, the shouting, and the thought came to him that it was a pity Asa Breen could not have been present to see the ovation they were giving to the *Western Star* and its gallant force. It might have repaid him for the hell of remorse he'd been through those last few days of his life. His boat had saved hundreds upon hundreds of lives.

Captain Wilks came in to shake hands with Brant. The slender army officer said quietly, 'I misjudged you up at Skull Cove, Captain, and I apologize. The Army owes you much for what you've done this day.'

'Your men made the fight,' Brant smiled. 'I took them to it.'

Ropes were being cast ashore now, and the *Western Star* snubbed to the wharf. Planks were shoved over the side, and the happy troopers disembarked.

Brant went below with Walt Carmody. He saw Charlie Barrett sitting on the guardrail of the texas, and the little scout nodded to him, and then shook his head sadly. Out of all the crowd assembled here, Brant realized, only the little scout gave one thought to the scattered Indian villages in which there would be mourning and wailing tonight for the dead. Only Charlie Barrett realized that an Indian was a human being.

Rock Monihan came out of the engine room, grinning, sweating as usual. He said to Brant, 'Didn't last too long, did it, Brant?'

'Not too long,' Brant answered.

He was looking for Laura Graham on the shore, and then he saw her, standing with Melodie Wade. When he crossed the planks with Walt Carmody and Rock Monihan, he walked straight toward her. He saw the happiness in her eyes as he approached.

Miss Wade was smiling, too. She said to Brant, 'I was sure you'd all come through it.'

Brant took Laura Graham's hand. He said to Melodie, 'You've met my fiancee, Miss Wade?'

He felt Laura squeeze his fingers as he said this, and Melodie Wade smiled at him happily.

'I'm so glad,' she said. 'Laura and I have gotten to know each other this evening.'

'She is going downriver with me,' Laura explained.

Brant glanced at Walt Carmody, who was standing by, hat in hand, and he saw the happiness come into the mate's eyes. On the long trip home Brant was sure Walt Carmody would waste no time as far as Melodie Wade was concerned, and he would have no rivals this trip.

Laura was saying, 'We're making a pot of coffee at the shop, Brant. We thought you and Walt would like to join us.'

'A pleasure.' Brant nodded. 'We'll be along in a few minutes. We have a little business to attend to first.'

He saw Walt Carmody glance at him curiously as he said this, and when they had said good-bye to the girls and were pushing their way through the crowd along the shore, Walt said to him, 'What is this business, Brant?'

'Do you have a gun?' Brant asked him quietly. He had a Colt .45 in his waistband which he'd put there before the *Western Star* headed for the sand bar.

'I have a gun,' Walt nodded.

'This a hunch,' Brant told him. 'Maybe I'm just curious.'

'About what?' the mate wanted to know.

'Shelby Flynn,' Brant murmured. 'I can't imagine him just walking off from this fight, leaving his warehouse and whatever valuables, gold dust and currency he might have in his warehouse and office in town.'

'You think he may have crossed over?' Walt asked softly.

'He wouldn't have too much trouble,' Brant said. 'There would be a boat or a canoe along the west bank, and with all the excitement here tonight he could easily slip into town and collect whatever he wanted to at his office without anyone particularly noticing him.'

'Kind of like to run into him,' Walt Carmody said softly. 'Reckon we owe him something, Brant.'

'Only a hunch,' Brant told him. 'Flynn might be heading west on the heels of the Indian bands by now.'

'More likely, though,' Carmody observed, 'that he'd collect whatever he could out of the mess he made, and head back to civilization.'

They reached the outskirts of the big crowd gathered along the shoreline, and they passed on through the silent streets, heading south now toward the warehouse. Neither man spoke as they moved swiftly along, turning back toward the river again after they'd walked three blocks.

As they came up to the warehouse it was in complete darkness, a long, low shed of a building, facing on the water.

'Looks empty,' Walt Carmody whispered, 'but then he wouldn't put any lights on if he was just comin' down here alone, hopin' nobody would see him.'

Brant didn't say anything. They moved around toward the rear door of the warehouse, feeling their way carefully. The stars were bright, glittering in the sky.

Brant tried the knob. It turned, and the first real hope came to him that they'd find Flynn in his warehouse. At this hour of the night a warehouse door would ordinarily be locked.

'He has a little office at the other end, facing on the river,' Walt Carmody whispered. 'I was in here once to buy some buffalo robes to take downriver.'

They passed into the building, closing the door softly behind them, and they stood in the darkness, both men drawing their guns. Then Walt touched Brant's arm.

'Light,' he said softly.

Brant saw the crack of light at the other end of the long room. The light undoubtedly came from a closed door.

'That's the office,' Carmody murmured. 'Reckon he's in there, Brant.'

Brant started to walk forward slowly, feeling his way around the boxes, crates and barrels in the room. It was a slow process because they didn't want to scare off their quarry by tripping over an object.

Foot by foot they drew nearer to the door. When they were within a few feet of it, Brant in the lead lifted his gun, steadied it, and then lunged forward, hitting the door with his shoulder. It had been locked from the inside, but the weight of Brant's body ripped the lock loose, and he lurched into the room. A lamp burned on the table, the wick turned down low.

There were two windows in the room, but the shades had been drawn down completely.

Shelby Flynn was there. He'd been walking toward the door which opened on the wharf, a bulging saddlebag under his arm, when Brant tumbled into the room. Flynn was unshaven, dirty, deep lines in his face. He looked totally unlike the smooth, immaculately dressed man Brant had known aboard the *Western Star*. Flynn had been living with Indians these past few days, and he looked it.

Seeing Brant come through the door, he whirled, his right hand going for the gun on his hip as he dropped the saddlebag. He was a wolf at bay here, savage, implacable.

Brant's first bullet hit him as the muzzle of his gun reached the height of Brant's waist. Flynn fired twice, but he was already falling, and his shots went wild. Brant continued to fire at him, steadily, deliberately, thinking of the women and the children in the town who'd nearly been slaughtered because of this man, thinking of all the good men in blue who'd gone under partly because of, Flynn's conniving. He shot at the man the way he would have shot at a mad dog, with only one thought in mind — to destroy him.

Flynn fell on his face, his hat rolling from his head. His shoulders quivered for a moment, and then he was still, and the dark stain of blood flowed from under him.

Walt Carmody said behind Brant, 'Why didn't you wait for me, Brant?'

'One target is better than two,' Brant murmured. He walked forward, bent down, and rolled Flynn over, looking into the dead face for a moment. Then he straightened up and said, 'That's it, Walt.'

'That's it,' Carmody nodded.

They stood there in silence. Upriver, they could hear the noise of the celebration at the *Western Star*'s berth. Downriver, a night owl hooted. The smell of the river came to them through the thin walls of the warehouse, dank and cool at night. It was the river upon which Brant McRae had been raised, and upon which he ran his own packet boat. It was a good river; it had had its baptism of blood this night, but it was a safe river now — one upon which a man could live and raise his family, and experience the full measure of happiness.

'Ready to go?' Walt Carmody asked.

Brant smiled. 'Ready,' he said briefly. He'd been ready a long time for that which lay ahead of him. He took the first step toward it as he left Flynn's warehouse.

We do hope that you have enjoyed reading this large print book.

Did you know that all of our titles are available for purchase?

We publish a wide range of high quality large print books including:
Romances, Mysteries, Classics
General Fiction
Non Fiction and Westerns

Special interest titles available in large print are:
The Little Oxford Dictionary
Music Book, Song Book
Hymn Book, Service Book

Also available from us courtesy of Oxford University Press:
Young Readers' Dictionary
(large print edition)
Young Readers' Thesaurus
(large print edition)

For further information or a free brochure, please contact us at:
Ulverscroft Large Print Books Ltd.,
The Green, Bradgate Road, Anstey,
Leicester, LE7 7FU, England.
Tel: (00 44) **0116 236 4325**
Fax: (00 44) **0116 234 0205**

MATCH RACE

Fred Grove

Quarter horse racing presents a thrill few men in the Old West can resist. Dude McQuinn, Coyote Walking, and Billy Lockhart are no exception, riding from town to town, matching and trading racehorses. Dude is the straight-talking front man, Coyote the jockey, and Billy the doctor, concocting potions that can cure a horse of anything — at least temporarily. But Billy is being watched by a strange man in a black bowler hat — a man who knows a secret about his past . . .